Dear reader,

MRS. GODFREY, HERE'S MY BOOK REPORT ON "MAX & THE MIDKNIGHTS"!

WHAT?

NATE, YOU WERE **SUPPOSED** TO READ A BOOK ABOUT **HISTORY**!

© 2019 Lincoln Peirce

IT **IS** ABOUT HISTORY! IT'S SET IN THE **MIDDLE AGES**!

AND IT'S CHOCK-FULL OF **GREAT CHARACTERS**!

MAX	THE MIDKNIGHTS	MUMBLIN
an apprentice troubadour	a merry band of misfits	a retired wizard

Yeah, but I **WANT** to be a **KNIGHT**!

MISFITS?

HONK.

Abra-KAZAM!

GASTLEY
a cruel king

OFF WITH EVERY-ONE'S HEAD!!

This book has everything: action, adventure, thrills, and tons of hilarious jokes!

ROARRR! There's even a genuine **DRAGON**!

THAT'S NOT HISTORY, YOU IDIOT! IT'S **FICTION**!

OH, AND THERE'S ALSO AN **EVIL WITCH** IN THE STORY!

SOUND LIKE ANYBODY YOU KNOW?

"MAX & THE MIDKNIGHTS" IS **MAGICAL**!

Nate Wright

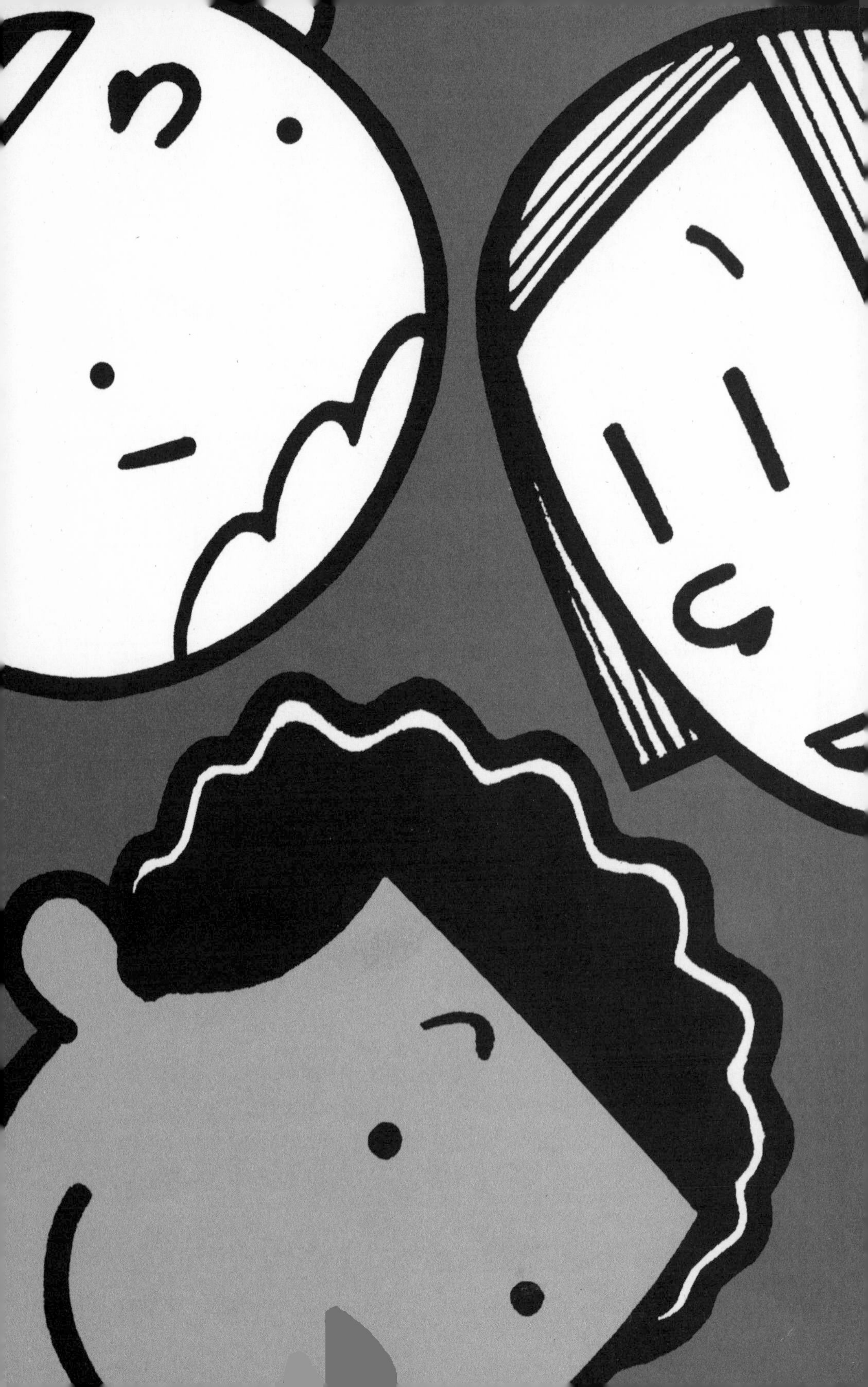

MAX
& the Midknights

Lincoln Peirce

CROWN BOOKS
for YOUNG READERS
New York

Copyright © 2019 by Lincoln Peirce

All rights reserved. Published in the United States by Crown Books for
Young Readers, an imprint of Random House Children's Books, a division
of Penguin Random House LLC, New York.

Crown and the colophon are registered trademarks of
Penguin Random House LLC.
Big Nate is a registered trademark of Scripps Licensing, Inc.

Visit us on the Web! rhcbooks.com

Educators and librarians, for a variety of teaching tools, visit us at
RHTeachersLibrarians.com

Library of Congress Cataloging-in-Publication Data
is available upon request.
ISBN 978-1-101-93108-0 (trade) — ISBN 978-1-101-93109-7 (lib. bdg.)
ISBN 978-1-101-93110-3 (ebook)

Printed in the United States of America

10 9 8 7 6

First Edition

For Jessica, Elias, and Dana

I'm going to tell you a secret: being a troubadour kind of stinks.

You know what troubadours are, right? They're traveling entertainers. And it's actually my uncle Budrick who's the troubadour, not me. He does all the singing and juggling. I'm just along for the ride.

You could call me his apprentice, I guess. I'm supposed to practice the lute (the instrument he's playing that looks like a giant chicken leg), learn all the songs, and prepare myself just in case Uncle Budrick sprains a tonsil. But here's the problem:

Why not? Well, you're on the road all the time, for one thing. That's a total drag. It's hard to make friends, too, because you're always moving from village to village. And this wagon we live in isn't exactly a four-star hotel. What else? Oh, yeah . . .

It's the MIDDLE AGES!

Yup, we're talking fourteenth century. That means a lot of important stuff hasn't been invented yet. Like paved roads, the toothbrush, and a little convenience known as indoor plumbing. It's a tough life, and—sorry, Uncle Budrick—I can't see how a few songs or some lame magic tricks will make it any easier.

See, here's how this troubadour thing is SUPPOSED to work: You roll into some random town. A crowd gathers. You put on a show. The crowd applauds and throws money in a basket. You take the money and use it to buy food and avoid starving to death.

Sounds simple enough, right? It's a basic business transaction. Except Uncle Budrick is a lousy businessman. He doesn't focus on the money. He gets distracted by other things, like . . .

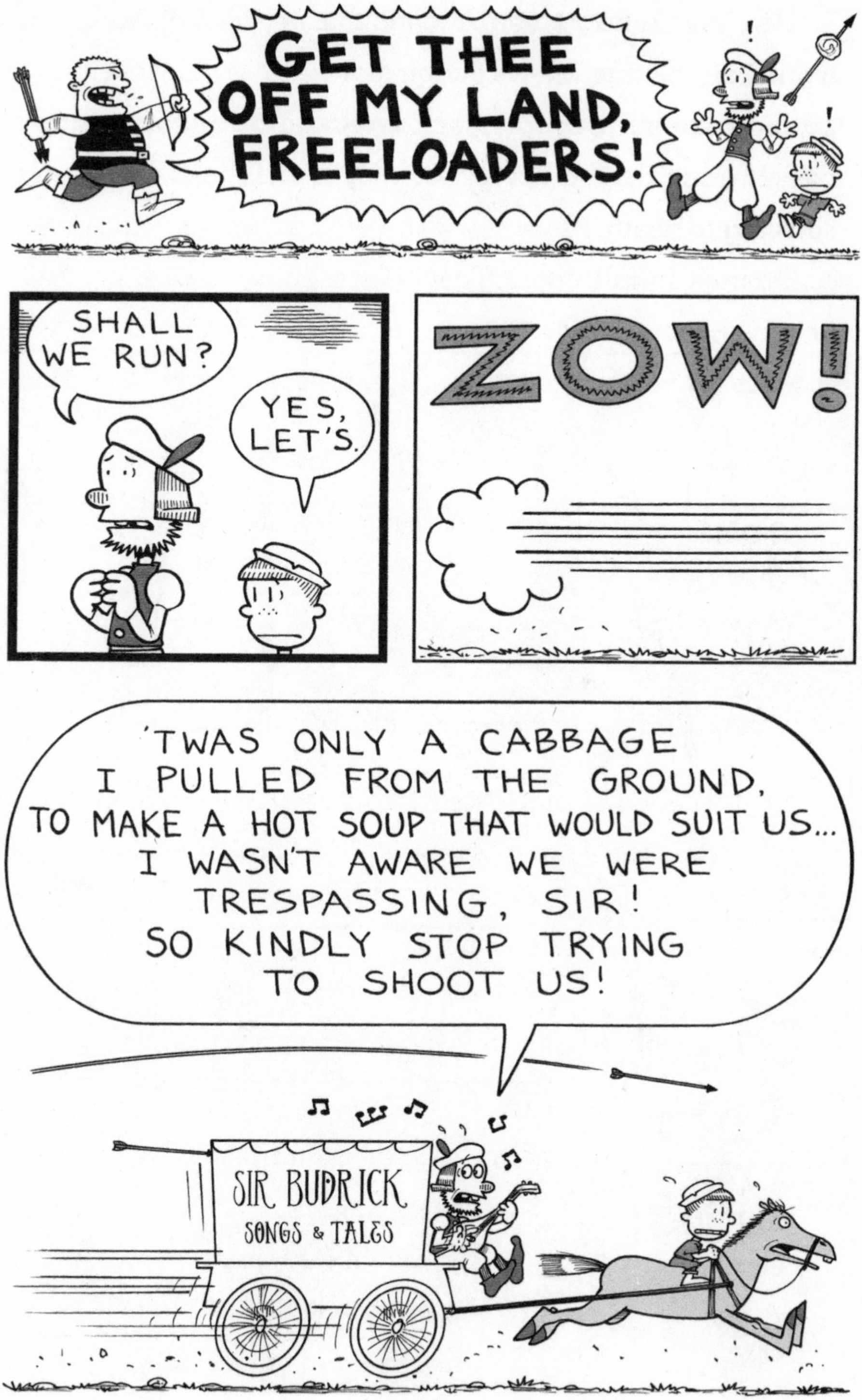
GET THEE OFF MY LAND, FREELOADERS!
!
!
SHALL WE RUN?
YES, LET'S.
ZOW!
'TWAS ONLY A CABBAGE I PULLED FROM THE GROUND, TO MAKE A HOT SOUP THAT WOULD SUIT US... I WASN'T AWARE WE WERE TRESPASSING, SIR! SO KINDLY STOP TRYING TO SHOOT US!
SIR BUDRICK
SONGS & TALES

This happens a lot. I don't mean that getting shot at is part of our daily routine, but we dodge more arrows than you might think. Apparently, people don't like strangers taking short-cuts through their property. Or maybe they just hate Uncle Budrick's singing. Anyway, by the time we manage to outrun Sir Bullseye back there, it's getting dark.

Sounds good to me. We slow to a stop in a grove of trees, and I unhitch the wagon. "Want me to build a fire?" I ask.

Uncle Budrick gives me a sheepish look. "I ... er ... dropped the cabbage when we made our getaway," he says. "There'll be no stew tonight, I'm afraid."

Uh . . . okay, I like the optimism, but . . .

Lucky for us, I happen to be a world-class tree climber. I scramble up into the tangle of branches while Uncle Budrick waits below.

"Oh, HO!" Uncle Budrick says, his voice growing excited.

Okay, THAT got my attention. "What do you mean, you HAD to leave?"

"Something unfortunate was about to happen," Uncle Budrick answers with a shudder. "If I'd stayed in Byjovia, Max, I very well might have become . . ."

Oops. That sounded kind of rude. But he's got to be pulling my leg, right? I mean, knights are supposed to be brave and strong and all that jazz. Uncle Budrick is—

As I was saying: Uncle Budrick is a total wuss bag.

"Well!" he says. "Shall we eat?"

"Not so fast," I tell him.

I WANT TO HEAR **MORE!**

HOW DID YOU ALMOST BECOME A **KNIGHT?**

LONG STORY.

PERHAPS THE BEST WAY TO EXPLAIN IT...

...IS WITH A **SONG!**

SUPER.

ZWIP!

♫ OHHHHHHH... ♫ LEND ME YOUR EARS AND I'LL—

PLOING!

NUTS.

BROKE A STRING.

"In Byjovia," Uncle Budrick begins, "when a young man turns ten, he has to start studying a trade. Most boys learn from their fathers. If your dad is a baker, you become a baker. If your dad is a miller, you become a miller."

"Well, MY dad was a knight," he continues, "but a very minor one. He wasn't much more than a squire, honestly. Anyway, he couldn't wait to enroll me in knight school."

My jaw nearly drops into the campfire. "They had a SCHOOL for KNIGHTS?"

Uncle Budrick nods. "They sure did. That's where they made you study all the knightly pursuits."

"Are you kidding?" I sputter. "WHY NOT??"

THINK OF THE **ADVENTURES** YOU COULD HAVE HAD!

Uncle Budrick shakes his head. "I wasn't interested in adventures, Max. I didn't want some dragon treating me like an after-dinner mint."

I NEEDED A WAY TO AVOID KNIGHT SCHOOL... AND I **FOUND** IT!

HOW?

"After watching him perform, I said to myself: THIS is a job that will put food on the table!"

"Because people were paying him money?"

"But the important thing was, he took me on as an apprentice! I left Byjovia and never looked back. My career as a troubadour had begun . . ."

Yes, I'm applauding. Compared to one of Uncle Budrick's sock puppet shows, that story was killer. "Do you ever wish you HAD become a knight?" I ask.

"Never," he replies. "Even at age ten, I knew I didn't want to."

"Certainly, my good fellow," Uncle Budrick says. "We have apples. Take as many as you'd like." He extends his hand, but the stranger doesn't shake it. Instead, he pulls something sharp and shiny from behind his back.

"Keep your rotten apples," he growls.

I can't believe this. "You're ROBBING us?" I exclaim.

BUT WE'VE GOT NOTHING TO **ROB!**

"The child is right, kind sir," Uncle Budrick squeaks. "We have no valuables. We are but humble troubadours!"

Uh...speak for yourself, big guy. YOU may be a troubadour, but I'M a...a...

WELL, I'M STILL FIGURING THAT OUT.

...BUT I'VE **GOT** TO BE SOMETHING MORE EXCITING THAN—

"HUMBLE TROUBADOURS"? DO YOU THINK ME A **FOOL?**

"Wh-what do you mean?" Uncle Budrick stammers.

SIR BUDRICK
SONGS & TALES

LOOK AT THE NAME ON YOUR **WAGON!**

THE ONLY PEOPLE WHO CALL THEMSELVES **SIR** ARE **KNIGHTS!**

Gulp. I don't like where this is going.

"And KNIGHTS are GOOD guys!" he continues. "Part of their job is chasing and capturing SCOUNDRELS..."

"You don't look much like one, that's certain," the stranger admits. "But I can't take any chances."

SO I'LL JUST GO AHEAD AND KILL YOU.

Whoa, did he say KILL? I thought this dirt ball just wanted to STEAL from us. Why spoil a perfectly good robbery by bringing MURDER into it?

No time to lose. I sneak a glance around our campsite for something to fight back with, but there's nothing. Just a few rocks and Uncle Budrick's lute. Then it hits me.

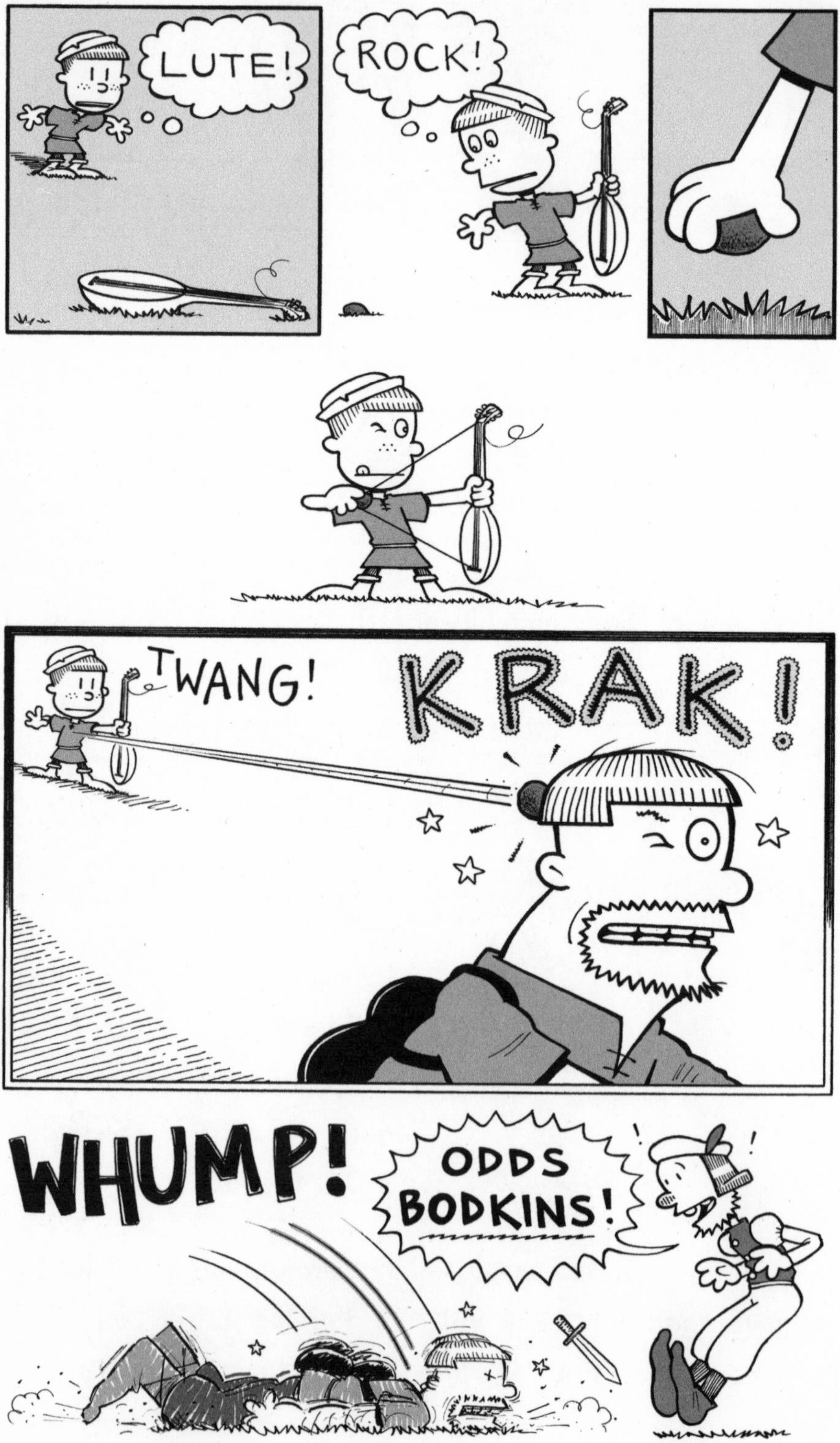
LUTE!
ROCK!
TWANG!
KRAK!
WHUMP!
ODDS BODKINS!

Wait, why am I suddenly acting all modest? The man's right. I AM incredible.

"How on earth did you do it?" Uncle Budrick asks.

Wow. Dusty's NEVER moved that fast. We stand there helplessly as his hoofbeats fade into the darkness. "NOW what do we do?" I ask.

"No waiting," I say, eyeballing the stranger on the ground. "Let's leave before Prince Charming here wakes up."

Uncle Budrick agrees. "Righto," he says, taking hold of the wagon. "Let's get rolling, Max. One . . . two . . . three . . ."

Yikes! Who nailed this thing to the ground? It won't budge. There's no choice but to continue on foot.

"Why do you want his dagger?" Uncle Budrick asks.

"Mostly so HE won't have it," I explain. "And now that it's mine, it's not a dagger anymore."

The moon is bright, so it's easy to see the road ahead of us. Still, it's tough going. These sacks are pretty heavy, and we're both exhausted. Which reminds me . . .

WHEN WE GET TO BYJOVIA, WHERE WILL WE **SLEEP?**

"I'm sure someone will give us shelter," Uncle Budrick replies. "The people of Byjovia are well-known for their warmth and friendliness."

THEY FOLLOW THE EXAMPLE OF THEIR **KING**...

CONRAD the KIND!

"Nice guy, huh?"

Uncle Budrick nods. "A good man. When I was a boy in Byjovia, he was beloved by everyone in the kingdom..."

...EXCEPT FOR ONE PERSON:

"What was Gastley peeved about?"

"He was jealous," Uncle Budrick answers. "As the firstborn son, Conrad inherited the throne. Gastley realized he'd never be more than a prince . . ."

"Yes, but nobody KNEW that," Uncle Budrick answers. "Gastley kept his nasty plans to himself—until one very memorable day in the market square."

YOU SEE, EVERY YEAR CONRAD HELD A CELEBRATION FOR THE PEOPLE OF BYJOVIA.

LONG LIVE KING CONRAD

THERE WERE LIVELY GAMES AND FROLICS.

THAT DAY, THE MAIN EVENT WAS...

...AN EXHIBITION OF **SKILLED SWORDPLAY!**

...FEATURING **KING CONRAD** AND **SIR GADABOUT!**

"Who was Sir Gadabout?"

"A royal knight. And the king's close friend."

"So they weren't having a REAL swordfight?"

"Not at all," Uncle Budrick says.

THEY WERE SIMPLY ENTERTAINING THE CROWD.

BUT THEN...

WHOOSH!

TIK!

EASY, OLD BEAN! YOU NEARLY **CLIPPED** ME!

HEY! LOOK AT THE **TREE**!

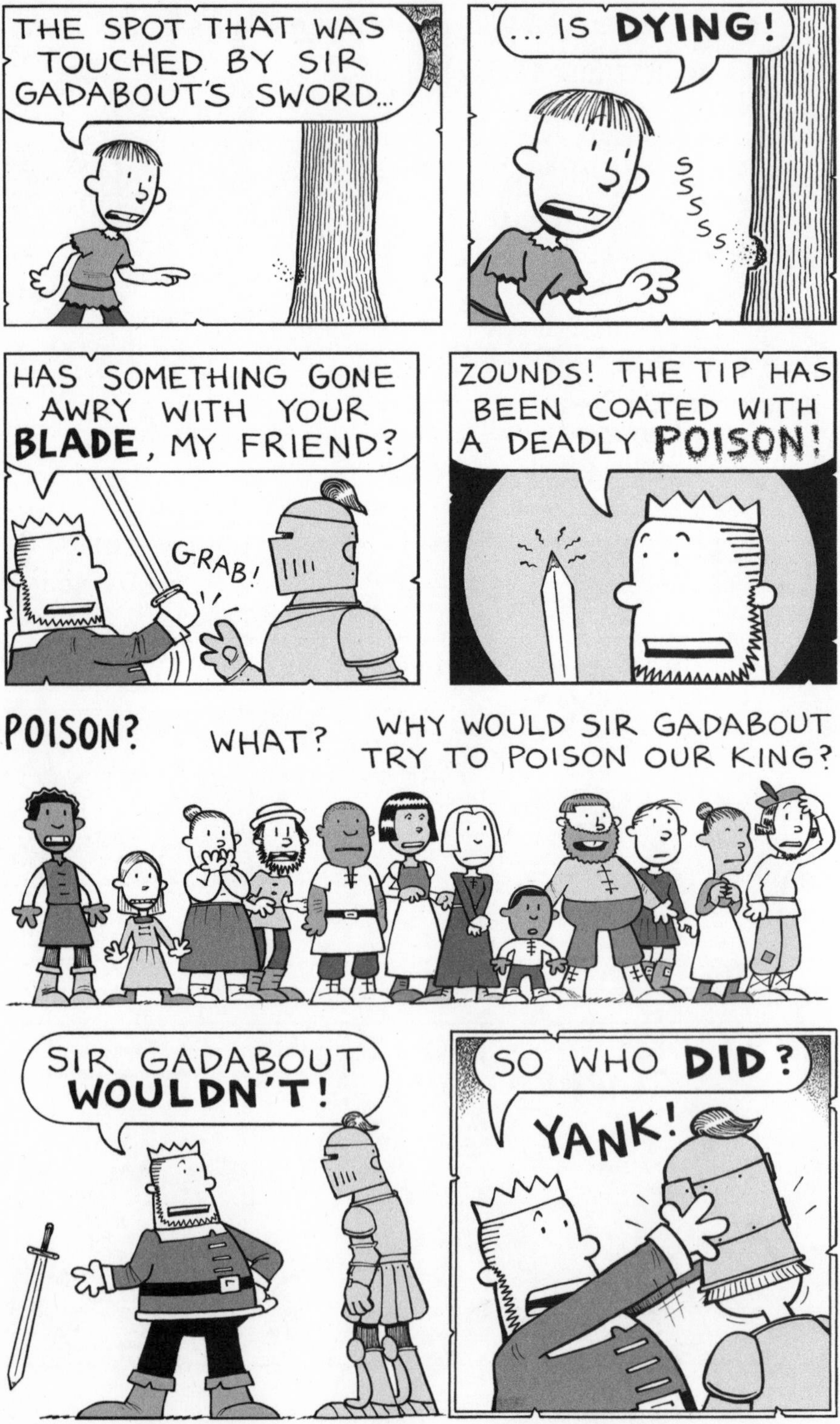

THE SPOT THAT WAS TOUCHED BY SIR GADABOUT'S SWORD...
... IS DYING!
SSSSS
HAS SOMETHING GONE AWRY WITH YOUR BLADE, MY FRIEND?
GRAB!
ZOUNDS! THE TIP HAS BEEN COATED WITH A DEADLY POISON!
POISON?
WHAT?
WHY WOULD SIR GADABOUT TRY TO POISON OUR KING?
SIR GADABOUT WOULDN'T!
SO WHO DID?
YANK!

"It was common knowledge that Gastley was a scallywag," Uncle Budrick says.

"No," he tells me. "Remember, he was Conrad the KIND."

"Speaking of Byjovia . . . ," I say.

"Let's stroll around a bit, Max," Uncle Budrick suggests.

I THOUGHT YOU SAID BYJOVIANS ARE **FRIENDLY**!

THEY **ARE**!

...OR THEY **USED** TO BE!

⊚ # ☀ ! ◎ ☆

BACK THEN, KING CONRAD PREACHED KINDNESS AND FELLOWSHIP!

WHAT'S CHANGED?

WELL... MAYBE CONRAD ISN'T KING ANYMORE!

HMM. GOOD POINT, MAX. I SUPPOSE THAT'S POSSIBLE.

"I think it's more than possible, Uncle Budrick," I tell him.

Uncle Budrick stares at the statue in surprise. "King Conrad is DEAD?" he cries. "But that's impossible! He was so young! He was only . . . um . . ."

Hmm, that's some fast math. Who's the whiz kid?

"And fifty-seven ISN'T young," the boy continues. "Remember, my good man, this is the fourteenth century!"

I have no idea what "salutations" are, but I guess it would be rude not to say anything. "My name's Max, and this is my uncle Budrick."

Kevyn grabs our hands and practically shakes us out of our shoes. "Delighted!" he gushes. "Charmed! Enchanted!"

"Robbed!" Kevyn echoes, his eyes widening. "Egad! How dastardly! So you have neither money nor lodgings?"

Suddenly Kevyn's as serious as a case of the plague. "Follow me," he whispers. And without another word, he darts down a nearby alley. We fall in behind, trailing him through a maze of crowded streets. Maybe I'm imagining it, but . . .

We duck through the tiny door of a modest wooden house. Once all three of us are inside, Kevyn exhales like a blacksmith's bellows. "Well done. We're safe here."

I'm not sure what we're safe FROM, but something tells me we can trust this kid. And we definitely need a rest. We drop the sacks from our aching shoulders and sit down.

"Calamitous is bad, right?" asks Uncle Budrick.

Kevyn nods. "If one of the Royal Guards had overheard you saying you were homeless and penniless..."

Wait, WHAT? First some jerk steals our wagon, and now we might get tossed in JAIL? That makes no sense. It's ... it's ...

"Outrageous!" Uncle Budrick fumes. "This is NOT the Byjovia I remember!"

"You're not alone in that opinion," Kevyn agrees. "My parents are similarly distressed."

Uncle Budrick leaps up like his pants are on fire. "But Gastley was banished from the kingdom! How could that skunk have possibly taken over?"

"Let me show you," Kevyn says. He zips into the next room and returns with a large scroll tucked under his arm.

THIS WILL ANSWER YOUR QUESTION!

The Tale of Byjovia

by Kevyn

The kingdom of Byjovia
Was prosperous and free.
The kindly Conrad ruled the land,
And all lived happily.

But news did reach King Conrad's ears
Of danger dark and foul.
Beyond the city's high stone walls
A beast was said to prowl.

Some claimed: "It is a monstrous wolf
With fangs that rip and maim!"
Some said: "It flies on dragon's wings
And burns the fields with flame!"

The panicked citizens cried out,
"Please, sire, protect our town!"
And so King Conrad ventured forth
To strike the creature down.

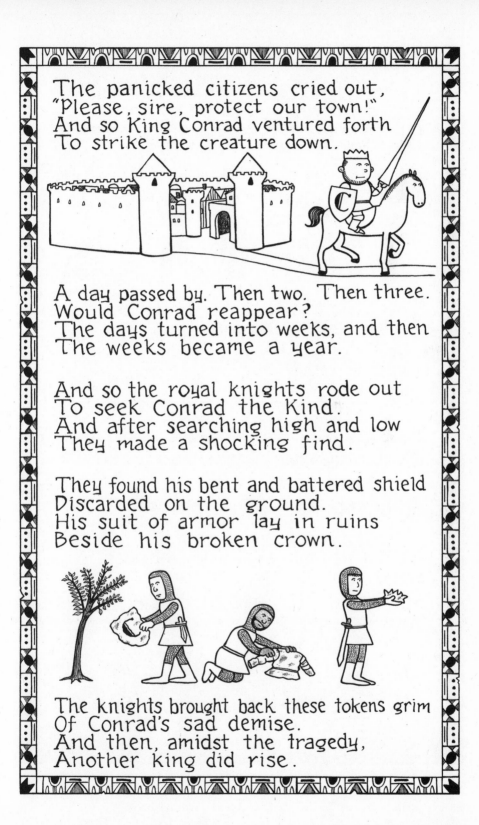

A day passed by. Then two. Then three.
Would Conrad reappear?
The days turned into weeks, and then
The weeks became a year.

And so the royal knights rode out
To seek Conrad the Kind.
And after searching high and low
They made a shocking find.

They found his bent and battered shield
Discarded on the ground.
His suit of armor lay in ruins
Beside his broken crown.

The knights brought back these tokens grim
Of Conrad's sad demise.
And then, amidst the tragedy,
Another king did rise.

The wicked Gastley had returned
To claim King Conrad's throne.
By show of force and point of sword,
He took it for his own.

The kingdom that had once been ruled
By one so pure and just
Now sank into a murky pit
Of anger and mistrust.

But do not let your heart despair!
Surrender not to fear!
For after every cold, black night
There dawns a morning clear.

King Gastley's reign will not endure.
His evil deeds will cease.
Byjovia will be reborn
In happiness and peace.

"What's that noise?" Uncle Budrick wonders.

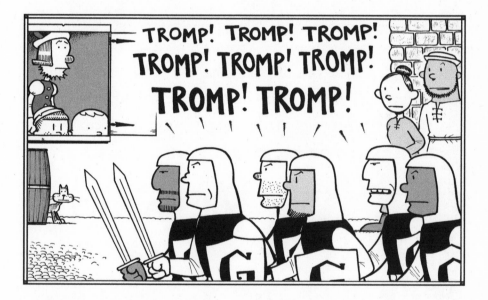

From the window, we watch a column of stone-faced soldiers march up the street in two straight lines. "Looks like a fun bunch of guys," I mutter.

"Those are the infamous Royal Guards," Kevyn whispers. "They accompany King Gastley wherever he goes."

"Well, if that's true," I say . . .

...GASTLEY MUST BE INSIDE THAT **WAGON!**

Kevyn corrects me, but in a nice way. "I believe it's called a coach, actually. And you're right, Max. The king is inside."

Not for long, though. The wagon—er, coach—rumbles to a sudden stop, and the door swings open.

ALL
HAIL
KING
GASTLEY!

YAAAAAY!!
CLAP CLAP CLAP CLAP
CLAP CLAP CLAP
CLAP CLAP CLAP
CLAP

"Why do the people cheer?" Uncle Budrick asks. "Don't they know what a WEASEL Gastley is?"

"They MUST cheer, or be thrown in prison," Kevyn answers. "But there's more to it than that, I'm sorry to say."

"Yes, I could feel that when we were walking on the street," Uncle Budrick notes.

Outside Kevyn's window, King Gastley stalks toward a nearby alley. Something's caught his eye.

The crowd moves aside, and I can see clearly who he's speaking to. It's a couple of kids. Their clothes are worn and tattered, and their feet are bare. I feel a nervous tingle in my stomach. Those two don't stand a chance.

The girl's voice trembles. "B-begging your pardon, Your Majesty. W-we left them at home."

"Oh, DID you, now?" Gastley jeers. He stares at her, his expression cold and mocking. "And where, pray tell, is this supposed home of yours?"

She falters. "It . . . it's . . . near the . . . um . . ."

The boy breaks in. He sounds defiant. "We have no home."

Gastley grins wickedly. "Ah! In other words . . ."

I can see what's coming. Gastley's goons are about to grab those kids and haul them off to the royal dungeon. And does anyone lift a finger to help? Nope. The people stand and stare like a flock of sheep.

By the time I'm a few feet away from the king, I'm having second thoughts about jumping into the middle of this. Half a dozen guards are facing me with their swords drawn, ready to turn me into a giant pincushion.

But they don't. With a lazy flick of his wrist, Gastley signals the men to fall back. Then he circles me like a hungry fox stalking a newborn chick.

"Well, WELL!" he sneers. "This is my lucky day! Here's ANOTHER filthy ragamuffin!"

Gastley moves closer to me, his foul breath stinging my nose. "Do you understand what I'm saying?" he hisses. "Take off your hat, boy. Or I'll take off your HEAD."

"Don't call me a boy," I tell him.

"Oh?" he growls. "And why not?"

"Because," I say . . .

There's a stunned silence. The crowd—from Kevyn to Gastley and everyone in between—seems totally shocked. What's WITH these people?

It's the king who speaks first. "Boy or girl, it makes no difference," he sniffs at me. "You're still a vagabond."

TAKE THIS ONE TO THE DUNGEON WITH THE OTHER TWO.

"Er ... Your Majesty," a soldier stammers, "the other two have run off."

Gastley's face turns a blotchy purple. "Then RUN AFTER THEM, you mutton-headed moron!" he bellows.

I'LL PUT THIS IMP IN A CELL **MYSELF!**

WAIT!

WAIT, I SAY!

Now it's MY turn to be shocked. Remember, Uncle Budrick has all the backbone of a baby snail. But here he is, standing up to the king in front of half of Byjovia.

Okay, forget that part about standing up. He's actually kneeling, which isn't quite as awesome. But let's see where this goes.

"Th-the girl is no vagabond, Your Highness," Uncle Budrick pleads. "She is with ME."

Gastley's lip curls with disdain. "And who are YOU?"

"M-merely an entertainer, Your Eminentness."

"You see, I currently find myself in need of just such a man!"

"Perhaps you misunderstood me, peasant," Gastley snaps.

The king smirks. "Bring him along to the castle," he orders his guards. "We'll see how amusing he is."

And with that, Gastley climbs back into his fancy-pants wagon and rolls away. The good news is, he's forgotten about me completely. The bad news is . . .

THEY'VE GOT MY **UNCLE!**

GASTLEY'S GOING TO TURN HIM INTO A **CLOWN!**

I'M GOIN' **AFTER** 'EM!

MAX! NO! **CONTROL** YOURSELF!

"You mustn't attempt a rescue on your own," Kevyn cautions me. "Gastley has an entire ARMY at his disposal!"

YOU'RE ONLY **ONE BOY!**

ER... I MEAN, **GIRL!**

I BEG YOUR PARDON, MAX! IT'S JUST THAT... THAT...

"That you thought I was a boy this whole time?" I say. "Well ... yes," he admits.

"It's okay, Kevyn, I'm used to it," I assure him. "Lots of people are surprised to find out I'm a girl."

"In all honesty, I was more surprised by the way you spoke to King Gastley," Kevyn tells me. "NOBODY has ever dared to confront him like that."

"You mustn't insult the king in public!" he whispers. "Gastley's spies are EVERYWHERE!"

I lower my voice. "Well, should I just stand around doing NOTHING?"

"Not necessarily!" Kevyn chirps. "As the royal fool, his task is to keep the king amused, correct?"

SO IF HE'S A GOOD ENTERTAINER, HE HAS NOTHING TO FEAR!

Fine, but what if he's NOT a good entertainer? I love Uncle Budrick, but I wouldn't put him in the Troubadour Hall of Fame. (There actually IS a Troubadour Hall of Fame, by the way. Worst gift shop ever.) The point is, Uncle Budrick won't be Gastley's fool for long. Once he runs through his song list and tells a few knock-knock jokes . . .

...HE'S IN TROUBLE.

KEVYN, WE'VE **GOT** TO HELP MY UNCLE!

"You're quite right," affirms Kevyn, his voice still hushed. "But it's perilous to discuss this in public."

? ?

COME. WE'LL GO TO THE STABLE.

"Why the stable?"

"My father works there," Kevyn answers. "He is an ostler."

Kevyn doesn't sound too happy about that, but before I can ask any questions, we've arrived. We swing open the large door and step inside, leaving the crowded street behind.

"Not exactly," Kevyn says. "I brought someone I'd like you to meet. Father, this is my friend Max."

Kevyn's dad has a friendly face, a thick, woolly beard, and—just now I notice it—a wooden peg where one of his legs should be. He smiles warmly as he shakes my hand. "Pleased to meet you, Max. I am called Nolan."

We quickly explain what happened to Uncle Budrick, and Nolan's smile hardens into a grim line. "So he's to be Gastley's jester," he mutters. "That's not a job I'd wish on anybody."

THE QUESTION IS, WHAT CAN WE DO TO —

HELP!

WE'RE BEING CHASED BY THE KING'S SOLDIERS!

THEY'LL BE HERE ANY MINUTE!

THEN WE MUST ACT QUICKLY!

UP IN THE LOFT WITH YOU, CHILDREN!

Nolan's voice is calm. "I assure you, there are no such people here. But you're more than welcome to look around..."

...IF YOU'RE WILLING TO **RISK** IT!

UH... WHAT DO YOU MEAN, "RISK IT"?

"One of my horses has fetlock fever," Nolan informs them. "If you come inside the stable, you'll likely be infected."

BUT DON'T WORRY! NOT **EVERYONE** DIES FROM IT!

DIES?

WITH ANY LUCK, YOU'LL ONLY GET OOZING PIMPLES ALL OVER YOUR—

YAAAAAH!!

I wait until the sound of the soldiers' boots fades into silence. Then I emerge from my hiding place.

THAT SURE GOT RID OF 'EM!

BUT FATHER! WHAT IF **WE** GET FETLOCK FEVER?

WE'RE SAFE, SON.

THERE'S NO SUCH THING AS FETLOCK FEVER!

WINK!

EGAD! YOU **OUTFOXED** THEM!

...AND YOU SAVED **US**!

HEY!

YOU'RE THE KIDS WE SAW ON THE STREET EARLIER!

AND **YOU'RE** THE BOY WHO STOOD UP TO THE **KING**!

- 61 -

"Might we stay here and rest for a little while?" Millie asks.

Millie turns pale. "Won't that be dangerous?"

Nolan chuckles. "I see you're a young woman of action, Max. But the castle is a fortress. It's surrounded by a moat, and the front gate is heavily defended. You can't force your way in."

Kevyn sighs. "Perhaps we're up a creek without a paddle . . ."

I examine the plain copper piece in Nolan's hand. "Er ... yup, that's a coin, all right," I confirm.

"Not just ANY coin!"

IT'S AN **ENCHANTED** COIN! GIVEN TO ME BY NONE OTHER THAN MUMBLIN the MAGICIAN!!

"Mumblin!" Millie exclaims. "The royal sorcerer to King Conrad! He was FAMOUS!"

"Uh ... wasn't the poor chap also the butt of countless jokes?" asks Kevyn.

HA! KEVYN SAID "BUTT"!

HE WAS SUPPOSEDLY THE MOST **INEPT** MAGICIAN **EVER!**

IS IT TRUE HE ONCE TURNED THE KING'S CROWN INTO A PIECE OF **BEEF JERKY?**

"He came to the stable many years ago," Nolan begins . . .

"And with that, he left!" Nolan concludes. "I put the coin away and forgot all about it . . ."

Nothing.

Nolan frowns. "I don't understand. I'm doing just as Mumblin instructed."

"Wait a second, you're only doing HALF of it!" I say excitedly. "Remember his exact words: 'HOLD THAT COIN TIGHT . . .'"

He's not kidding. As it rolls to a stop on the stable's dirt floor, the coin glows like a fiery ember, and the air around it seems to vibrate with tiny slivers of flickering light. I don't know what's happening . . .

. . . but I think we're about to see something spectacular!

I hear a low hum, like the buzzing of a hidden beehive. It grows louder and louder, until the ground seems to vibrate beneath my feet. Then . . .

Nolan picks up the coin. "You mean . . . this isn't one of a kind?" he asks, sounding a bit disappointed.

"I'm here, and I'm wet," Mumblin grouses.

"When you say you're a bit rusty," Kevyn wonders, "what exactly are you implying?"

"That my career is over," Mumblin explains. "After King Conrad's unfortunate disappearance, I gave up my position as the royal wizard and retired from the magical world. I moved to the Shady Acres Home for Aged Sorcerers."

"But you CAN'T be retired!" I protest. "We need your help!"

Mumblin's clearly startled when he spots the gleaming dagger in my hand.

He takes it from me and gazes at it intently, brushing a wrinkly finger along a series of markings etched in the handle. "Where did you get this, boy?"

"I'm not a boy," I say for about the fiftieth time today.

Uh ... could WHAT be? I'm not sure what's going on, but Mumblin's forgotten all about the dagger. Instead, he's focused on yours truly. The guy's staring at me like I have two heads.

"Tell me, young lady," he says after a long pause.

The old wizard seems lost in thought. Finally, he shakes his head as though rousing himself from a deep sleep. "I have made a decision," he announces.

"You can thank me, Max, by finding me some food," he replies. "I didn't get much to eat at Shady Acres this morning."

"We'll need to avoid any of Gastley's guards that might be lurking about," Kevyn reminds us.

"You weren't going to help us at first, and now you are," I continue. "What changed?"

Mumblin strokes his beard. "I have my reasons, Max. And I promise to share them with you at the appropriate time."

We step out onto the street. Nolan and Mumblin walk ahead, and the rest of us follow at a short distance.

"You don't want to be an ostler, do you?" I ask him.

Kevyn's voice is flat. "It doesn't matter what I want, Max."

"But if you COULD do whatever you wanted," Millie says . . .

WHAT WOULD YOU DO?

His expression brightens. "Well," he answers, almost whispering . . .

"Like the one you showed me at your house!" I remind him.

"Yes," Kevyn agrees. "But that was a cloth scroll. A book is written on sheets of paper."

"Wow," Simon marvels. "Books sound . . . FANTASTIC."

"They are." Kevyn sighs. "But there's no sense talking about this any longer."

I'M TO BE AN OSTLER...

...AND THAT'S THE END OF IT.

Poor Kevyn. No wonder the two of us get along so well. He wants to write books, I want to be a knight, and we're both stuck doing other things.

Nolan leads us into the house, and I think of Uncle Budrick. We were together in this room only hours ago.

NOW... WHO **KNOWS** WHERE HE IS?

DEAR HUSBAND!

A cheery-looking woman with a sunny smile hugs Nolan.

THAT'S MY MOM!

I THOUGHT IT MIGHT BE.

"We have guests, my dear!" Nolan says. "Everyone, please allow me to introduce my wife, Alice!"

Alice beams. "What else would you be?"

"Well, most people think I'm a boy," I explain. "I've tried dressing more ladylike once or twice, but it's tough to run or ride a horse in a skirt."

"I quite agree, Max," she says with a laugh. "And I think your clothes suit you perfectly."

I like this woman already.

The four of us gather around the fireplace, where Mumblin
is ... uh ... well, he's snoring like a troll with a head cold.

"Wha—? The Castle! Yes! Of course!" Mumblin wheezes,
waking up from his mini-coma. "I was just ... er ... meditating
on that very subject!"

"And?" all of us ask in unison.

"Our strategy will depend on how Gastley defends the front gate," Mumblin says.

THERE MAY BE ARMED GUARDS...

...OR FIERCE ATTACK DOGS...

". . . or perhaps even some manner of exotic beast!"

...LIKE A GOBLIN, A WEREWOLF, A GRIFFIN, A DRAGON, A LABRADOODLE...

LABRA-DOODLE?

SUPPER IS READY!

We bolt to the table. An hour later, after the best meal I've ever eaten, I'm ready to take on anything Gastley throws at us. Even a labradoodle.

KEVYN, WILL YOU SHOW SIMON AND ME THE STORY YOU WROTE?

"THE TALE OF BYJOVIA"? SURELY!

MEANWHILE, **I'LL** CLEAN THESE DIRTY DISHES... WITH **MAGIC!**

LOVELY!

CRASH!

WHOOPS.

Alice and I sit down by the fireplace. "Thank you for telling us a bit about yourself during supper, Max," she says. "Being an aspiring troubadour is an uncommon way of growing up!"

YEAH, IT'S UNCOMMON, ALL RIGHT.

BUT I'M NOT AN ASPIRING TROUBADOUR. NOT REALLY.

OH? YOU'D RATHER HAVE A **DIFFERENT** JOB?

"Not if it means leaving Uncle Budrick," I say quickly. "But once we get him away from that pinhead Gastley . . ."

Alice's smile flickers briefly, and for just a moment she looks a little sad.

"I think that's a wonderful idea," she says. "But, Max, there's something I have to tell you."

"WAIT a minute!" I protest. "Don't girls get to learn a trade like BOYS do?"

"Yes, but not the SAME trades," Alice replies. "Girls usually become seamstresses or midwives or milkmaids or—"

"I don't WANT any of those jobs!" I insist.

"Um . . . yeah," I admit. "But I'm not doing that for the THRILL of it or anything. I'm doing it so he'll be SAFE!"

"I know you are, Max," Alice says gently.

"We're coming with you," Simon declares.

Huh? I wasn't expecting this. I knew Kevyn was on board, but I never thought Simon and Millie would offer to help.

They haven't even MET Uncle Budrick.

"If not for you, Max, Simon and I would probably be locked in the royal dungeon right now," Millie tells me.

"And besides," Kevyn adds, "everyone knows knights are most effective when they're working in GROUPS!"

"It isn't pretending," I point out. "We're breaking into the castle for REAL."

"I've got it!" Kevyn cries. "The perfect name!"

"The Midknights!" Simon repeats, his eyes shining. "I like it!"

"Good luck . . . and please be careful," Alice whispers. She's worried, and I don't blame her. But we'll be okay. I hope.

We inch along the streets single file. It's unbelievably dark, and in the air there's the smell of . . . of . . .

The castle rises above us like an enormous mountain, and the towers look like peaks outlined against the night sky. Nolan peers through the darkness at the front gate, straining to see what waits for us there.

"Something just moved," Nolan murmurs.

"Um . . . how could gargoyles MOVE?" Kevyn asks.

Mumblin's words send a chill down my back. BROUGHT TO LIFE. Meeting up with a moving, breathing, possibly girl-eating chunk of granite doesn't sound like much fun. But let's try to think positively.

"We need to get closer," Simon whispers. We shuffle forward until they come into view. Two massive figures crouch by the castle entrance. Their faces look like freakish masks, and their limbs are the size of tree trunks.

He's THINKING? Gee, that's helpful. While he's racking his brains, my uncle's head could wind up in Gastley's trophy case. I can't wait around for some second-rate wizard to have an aha moment. I've got to DO something.

We creep steadily toward the gate, hiding ourselves in the inky shadows of the buildings lining the street. Drawing nearer, I notice the gargoyles' massive heads slowly turning as they scan the night air. But they haven't spotted us.

It sounds pretty cool—until the bolt of light from Mumblin's wand arcs slightly, bounces off a rock near the castle gate, and . . .

Great. Here we are, trying to break into this sneak-proof castle, and the guy who's supposed to be our secret weapon just turned himself into a giant lawn gnome.

ROARRR!!

THEY'RE GOING TO EAT ME FIRST BECAUSE I'M HUSKY.

OOF! I DON'T THINK I CAN OUTRUN THEM!

YOU DON'T **NEED** TO!

YOU TAKE MUMBLIN BACK TO THE HOUSE! **WE'LL** HANDLE THE GARGOYLES!

WE WILL?

YUP.

Notice I didn't say HOW. Frankly, I have no idea what I'm doing. But if the four of us are going to save Uncle Budrick, I'd better think of something.

"We need to approach this like knights," I say as Big and Ugly come thundering toward us.

I nod. "You're right. We have none of that stuff."

We sprint to a nearby cluster of empty barrels. "Grab one and get in," I holler. "NOW!"

Sorry to sound bossy, but when you're about to be a snack for a couple of gargoyles, it's okay to forget your manners.

There's no turning back now. In fact, there's no turning, PERIOD. Ever try to steer a rolling barrel? All we can do is close our eyes and hope we hit our target.

I know, I know—an old wooden barrel won't hold a gargoyle for long. But we don't need it to last forever.

Holy cow. So this is the royal castle. I was expecting it to be roomy, but this is ridiculous. It's GINORMOUS.

There's no place to hide in this corridor. We scoot through the nearest door and find ourselves in a giant dining hall.

Kevyn and Simon duck behind a tapestry on the wall. Millie and I dive under the table. A heartbeat later, two of Gastley's swordsmen come marching in.

"We're supposed to report to the king's throne room," one of them says. "Why are we stopping here?"

"Because I'm HUNGRY, you idiot," the other one barks.

The first man leaves. Now the only sound in the room is the second guy, smacking his lips noisily as he inhales everything on the table. Maybe we'll get lucky and this dope will choke on a chicken bone.

Not if I have anything to say about it. I can take this guard by surprise if I use my dagger and—

Max, you DUNCE! What kind of a knight goes on a dangerous mission and forgets to bring a weapon? I leap to my feet and quickly scan the tabletop. There has to be something here I can use. A knife. A fork.

Hmm, this is tricky. If I answer, he'll know from the sound of my voice that I'm half his size. But I can't say NOTHING. I take a deep breath and set my vocal cords to "macho."

I'd know that voice anywhere. A little off-key—okay, a LOT

off-key—but believe me, it's music to my ears.

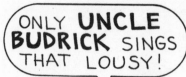

ONLY **UNCLE BUDRICK** SINGS THAT LOUSY!

IT'S COMING FROM OVER THERE.

On tiptoes, we approach a gleaming golden door. It's open just a crack. We nudge against it and slip inside.

A couple of guards stand nearby, but they're not looking our way. They're watching the scene in the center of the room.

My heart sinks. So this is what it means to play the fool. Poor Uncle Budrick looks exhausted. He's dressed in a moth-eaten clown costume, and as he performs a clumsy two-step in front of Gastley, he stumbles and nearly falls.

"Stop," Gastley demands. "STOP!"

YOU STINK!

A FOOL IS SUPPOSED TO KEEP THE KING **ENTERTAINED!**

INSTEAD, YOU GIVE ME A STUPID SONG ABOUT SOME FILTHY **PIG**!!

"I . . . I hoped you might find it amusing, Your Majesty," Uncle Budrick stammers.

"Amusing? No," Gastley scoffs. "BORING, yes. I'm afraid you're simply not very good at your job, old boy."

BUT DON'T FRET! I HAVE A **SOLUTION** TO THIS VEXING PROBLEM!

Y-YOU DO?

INDEED.

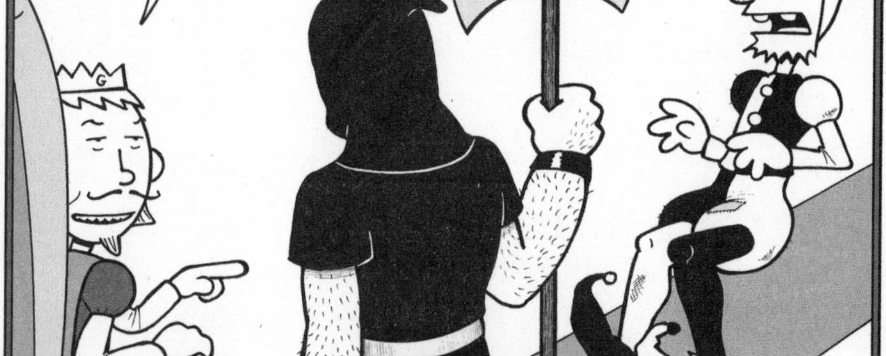
OFF WITH HIS HEAD.
G

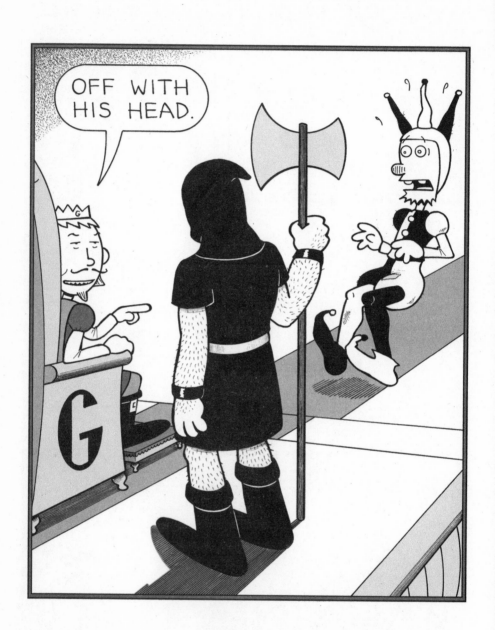

7

I feel my knees buckle, but I steady myself. I can't faint like some prissy princess who just found a fly in her porridge. Uncle Budrick needs me. He needs ALL of us.

Gastley can't hide his surprise as I skid to a stop on the marble floor. "YOU again," he snarls. "What is this?"

Good question. I'm just making this up as I go along. But there's no way I'm admitting that to his royal dorkship.

"Uh . . . you're being unfair to this man!" I finally blurt out.

Gastley gives Kevyn a dismissive wave. "I have seen juggling before," he growls.

"Not like THIS!" Kevyn continues. "We are renowned for

the astounding variety of items we juggle! Eggs! Flaming torches! Orange marmalade!!"

"Swords?" Gastley repeats. NOW he's interested. He licks his lips greedily. "I daresay, such a bold display could be rather . . . DANGEROUS."

And that's when we know that Gastley's not just mean—he's stupid, too. We can hardly believe our eyes as all his goons disarm themselves and hand over their weapons.

Gastley's bloodless face goes scarlet as he realizes he's just made a king-sized blunder. "You have TRICKED me!" he shrieks.

"Yeah, sorry about that," I say, my sword still pointing straight at his royal belly button. "But it's only fair, don't you think? You turned my uncle into a fool . . ."

We sprint toward the doorway. I steal a glance over my shoulder and see Gastley pick up a giant mallet. He swings it hard against a silver gong, and the air seems to vibrate with the sound of it.

I guess we forgot that the jokers who gave us these swords aren't Gastley's only guards. He's got a castle full of 'em. And they're catching up to us.

We rush through another set of doors. There's a cool blast of air on my face, and looking up, I see the moon glowing in the night sky. We're in some sort of outdoor courtyard, surrounded on all sides by towering stone walls.

Gastley's bruisers come charging into the courtyard, blocking the only way out. This doesn't look good. Sure, we've still got swords . . . but so do they. And unlike us, they actually know how to use them.

TONNG!

See what I mean? Who even knew it was possible to CUT A SWORD IN HALF? We can't compete with these guys. Stay tuned for the shortest battle ever.

And then I hear them: two distinct noises that ring through the air and rattle the ground.

What IS that? All of us—Midknights and soldiers alike—lower our swords and listen as the sounds draw nearer. Boom. Clack. BOOM. CLACK. BOOM ...

A gigantic wooden column crashes to the ground beside us. It's as if a massive tree fell from the sky and landed upright in the courtyard. But this is no tree.

It's a LEG.

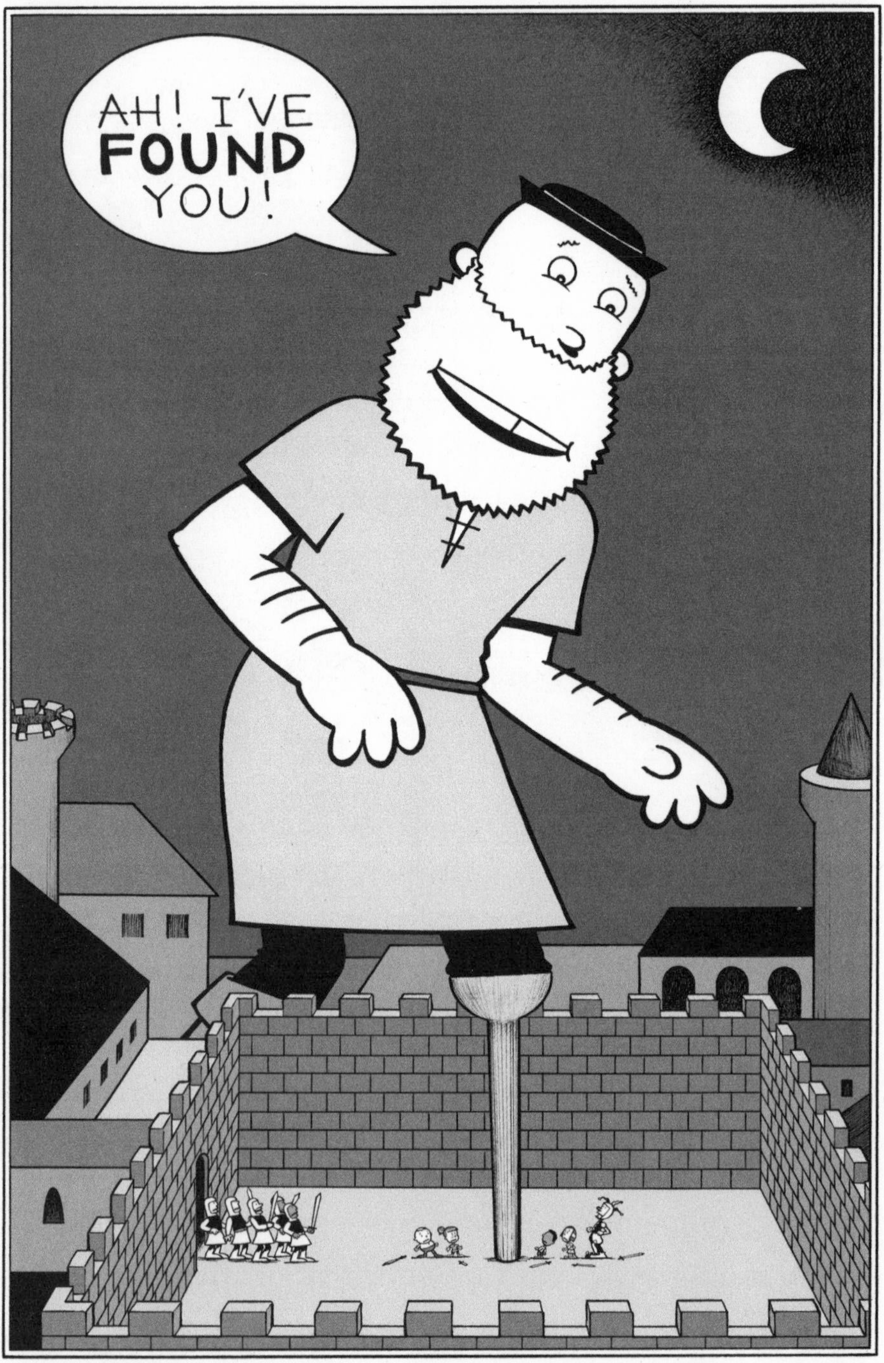
AH! I'VE FOUND YOU!

Quick reminder: about an hour ago, Kevyn's dad was six feet tall. Now he's TEN TIMES that. When he speaks, his voice rumbles like a clap of thunder.

In one swift motion, Nolan scoops us up, lifts us high above the rooftops, and drops us safely in the brim of his cap—which is fine for everyone except Uncle Budrick.

Gastley's men make a hopeless attempt to chop Nolan down with their swords, but he gently swings his wooden leg across the courtyard and sends them sprawling. Then he steps carefully back over the wall and tiptoes away from the castle, his foot and peg echoing more quietly now. Boom. Clack. Boom. Clack.

Sure enough, it's a short trip. After just a few minutes, Nolan sets us down in the alley behind Kevyn's house. And guess who's there to greet us?

MUMBLIN!

THE LAST TIME WE SAW YOU, YOU WERE A **STATUE**!

INDEED I WAS, MAX!

BUT LIKE MANY A MAGICIAN, I HAVE A **FAIL-SAFE**!

"IN CASE OF EMERGENCY, PRESS HERE."

"Nolan discovered that button while carrying me to safety," Mumblin explains, "and the petrification spell was broken!"

OH! SPEAKING OF SPELLS...

I NEED TO CUT YOU DOWN TO **SIZE**!

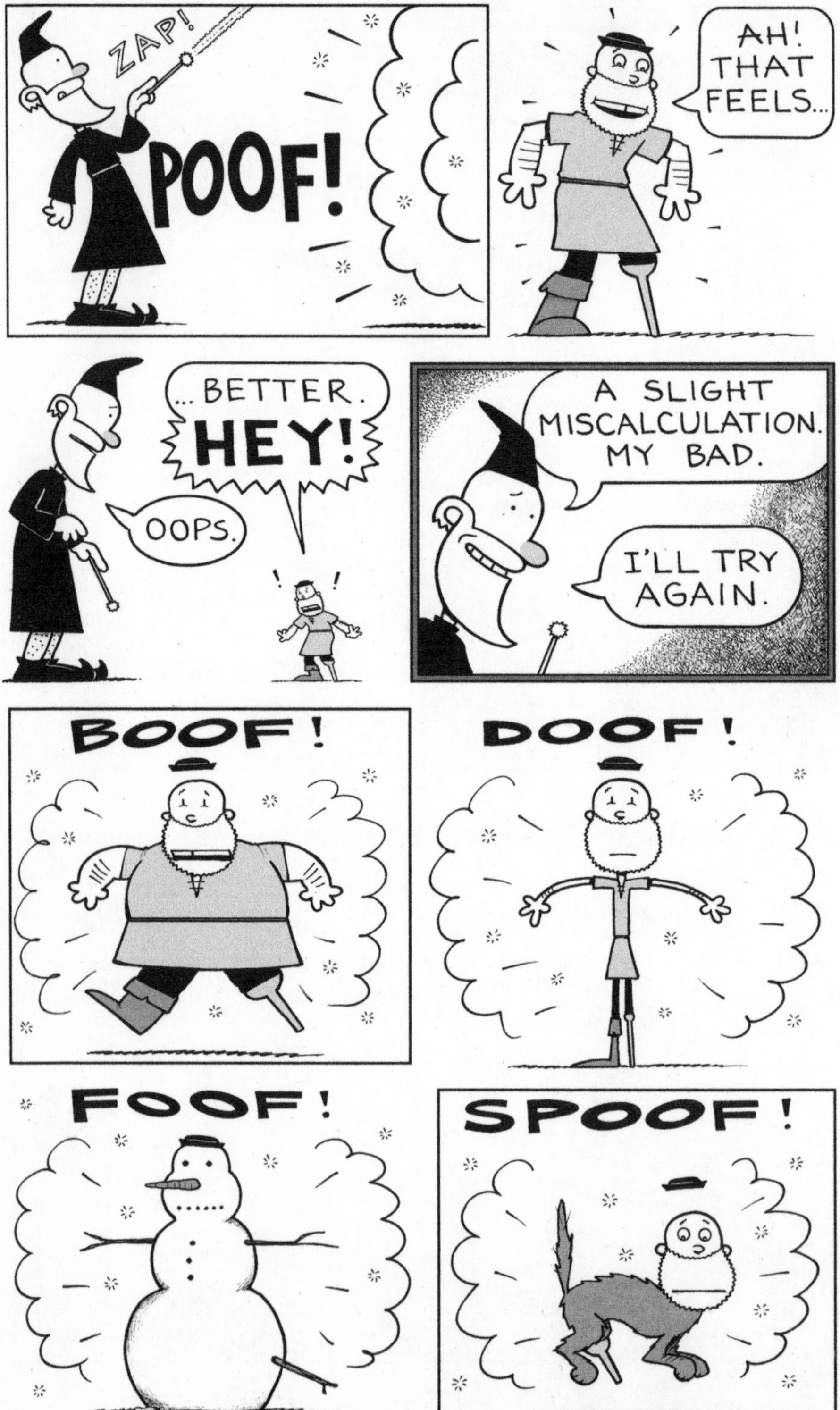

ZAP!
POOF!
AH! THAT FEELS...
... BETTER.
HEY!
OOPS.
! !
A SLIGHT MISCALCULATION. MY BAD.
I'LL TRY AGAIN.
BOOF!
DOOF!
FOOF!
SPOOF!

"Even if your powers are a bit wonky," Simon tells Mumblin, "you did it! You saved us from Gastley!"

UGH! IT'S **GASTLEY!**

HIS ROYAL **WEASELNESS!**

HEY, WHAT'S THAT HE'S HOLDING?

REWARD
for the
capture of

This
man

A **WANTED POSTER!** THAT'S **YOU**, UNCLE BUDRICK!

OH, COME **ON!** MY NOSE IS **NOT** THAT BIG!

"He'll hang those posters all over the kingdom," Nolan warns. "There will be no place to hide in Byjovia."

THEN... WE'LL **LEAVE** BYJOVIA.

✳SIGH.✳ UNCLE BUDRICK AND I ARE USED TO BEING ON THE ROAD.

YES! WE'LL GO BACK ON THE TROUBADOUR CIRCUIT AND PUT THIS WHOLE STORY BEHIND US!

Mumblin strokes his beard. "I agree that you should leave Byjovia. But I'm afraid you can't put this story behind you."

"Why not?" I ask.

The old wizard reaches into the folds of his cloak and pulls out a bent and battered book. "Because the story is about YOU, Max . . ."

A sudden thrill shoots through me. Whatever Mumblin is talking about, it sure sounds more exciting than being an apprentice troubadour.

"You mean . . . it predicts the future?" Millie asks.

He nods. "These pages have accurately foretold every major event in the history of the kingdom."

"Quite a bit, Max," Mumblin replies.

"Not by name," Mumblin tells me. "But based on my careful reading of the text, I'm certain it refers to you."

"How do you even know what it says?" Kevyn asks, flipping through the weathered pages.

"Rats," Kevyn grumbles.

"The Book of Prophecies was created by ancient sorcerers," Mumblin goes on. "For generations, the royal magicians of Byjovia were its caretakers."

A wicked man will rule the land
And call the crown his own.
But if our realm is to survive,
He must be overthrown.

One day a rescuer will rise
To set our kingdom free.
This hero's name will be a boy's,
But lo! A girl she'll be.

A mane of ginger hair she'll have
With eyes of sparkling jade.
And in her small but steadfast hand
She'll hold a royal blade.

A journey she will undertake.
Great courage she will need.
She must employ both Man & Boy
If she is to succeed.

Uncle Budrick sounds skeptical. "You think that's MAX?"

"It could be talking about ANY girl," I add. "Plus, I don't have a 'royal blade.'"

"Yes, you do," Mumblin counters. "Your DAGGER."

"How can that be?" I protest. "I took this from a BANDIT we met on the road!"

"Then he must have found it—or stolen it—long before you encountered him. That's not important."

WHAT MATTERS IS THAT **YOU** HAVE IT NOW!

EGAD, MAX! DON'T YOU **SEE?** A GIRL WITH A BOY'S NAME! GINGER HAIR! JADE EYES!

THE PASSAGE THAT MUMBLIN READ FITS YOU TO A **T**!

KEVYN IS RIGHT! THERE CAN BE NO DOUBT ABOUT IT!

MAX, **YOU** ARE THE HERO DESCRIBED IN THE BOOK OF PROPHECIES!

!!!

My head is spinning. Rescuing Uncle Budrick was tough enough. Now some moldy book says I'm going to bring down Gastley? Sorry if this sounds unheroic, but . . . HOW?

"What am I supposed to do?" I ask. Be specific, people.

"There are a few more lines here that might prove helpful," Mumblin says, opening the book again.

Four others will accompany
Our hero on this day.
When they take flight
At dawn's first light...
The blade shall point the way.

"Hear that, Max?" Simon chirps.

"Four others!"

THAT MEANS THE **MIDKNIGHTS** ARE COMING **WITH** YOU!

BUT THAT'S ONLY **THREE** OTHERS!

BUDRICK WILL BE THE FOURTH... FOR HIS OWN SAFETY!

DON'T FORGET, THE KING WANTS HIM **DEAD**!

THANKS FOR THE REMINDER.

IF YOU'RE TO LEAVE AT DAWN, WE HAVE NO TIME TO WASTE!

We all leap into action. Alice finds some proper clothes for Simon and Millie. Nolan fills our traveling sacks with food and supplies. Uncle Budrick changes out of his clown costume.

Mumblin whips out his wand with a flourish. "Leave this to me! Disguises are my specialty!"

ZAP!

I GOTTA TELL YA, I DON'T FEEL VERY DOGGY.

DUDE. YOU'RE A **GOOSE!**

THAT WOULD EXPLAIN MY SUDDEN URGE TO FLY SOUTH.

ARRGH! **DARN** IT!

THIS BLASTED THING IS BEYOND REPAIR!

TOSS!

Mumblin's wand clatters to the floor at Millie's feet.

IF YOU'RE DONE WITH THIS, MAY **I** KEEP IT?

OF COURSE, MY DEAR!

BUT REMEMBER, IT HAS OUTLIVED ITS USEFULNESS! IT'S NOW MERELY A **STICK!**

Millie is more stunned than anyone. "I don't know how I did that," she whispers.

"I'll tell you how you did it!" Simon crows.

"People discover their powers at different times," Mumblin explains. "I myself realized I was unusual almost from BIRTH."

Kevyn's standing by the window. Peering past him, I notice an orange glow creeping into the night sky. It's almost sunrise. But that's not what he's looking at.

Gastley's guards are lumbering up the street, scouring the dark alleys and pounding their fists on every door.

Wow, is this weird. My uncle—who's now a GOOSE—is Byjovia's most wanted man. We'd better get our tail feathers out of here, and fast. Otherwise, we're all dead ducks.

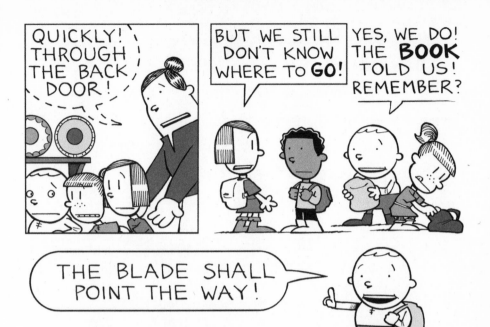

We scurry from the kitchen into the tiny back alley.

"Hand me your dagger, Max," Nolan says, and places it gently on the cobblestones beneath our feet. "I'll SPIN it, and whichever direction it's pointing when it stops . . ."

We all watch as the blade whirls like a top—quickly at first, and then slower and slower until it finally comes to rest.

"That's true north," Nolan murmurs. "Follow the cow path beyond the orchard. It will lead you in the right direction."

I try to ignore the knot forming in my stomach. This all seems so crazy. Heroes are supposed to begin their adventures with banners waving and people cheering . . .

And that's it. The five of us make our way up the alley. I take a final look over my shoulder before we turn the corner. Nolan, Alice, and Mumblin have already faded into the shadows.

There's not much to tell you about the first leg of our journey. By night, we sleep in haystacks or under trees. By day, we hike. And hike. And hike some more.

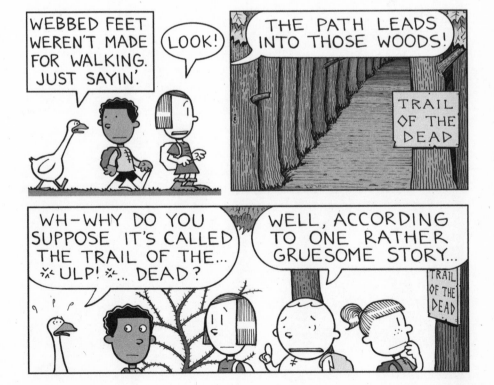

"Let's skip the gruesome stories," I say.

We start walking. It's just a regular path at first, but before long the ground becomes rough and uneven. The bushes and brambles edge closer to the trail, and the trees overhead seem to grow thicker, blocking out all but a few traces of sunlight. It starts to feel cold. REALLY cold.

"They remind me of gravestones," Simon whispers, "but they don't have any writing on them."

The ground beneath the stones is moving, soil and mud pushing upward as though an earthquake has suddenly begun. There's a muffled roar from below the surface. A hand appears— a gruesome, grasping hand with skin the color of swamp water.

And then the earth breaks open.

Yes, and they're heading this way. My heart pounding, I reach for Conrad's dagger. Simon is armed, too, with a knife that Nolan gave him when we left Byjovia. But these aren't exactly broadswords we're holding. They feel more like a couple of limp noodles.

I wish Mumblin were here. Wait—no, I don't. The old goat would probably turn himself into a jelly doughnut. And besides, he doesn't even have a WAND anymore. He gave his old one to . . . to . . .

Millie pulls the wand from her pocket as the trio of corpses comes lumbering toward us. "Use it HOW?" she cries. "I don't know any spells!"

"MAKE ONE UP!" screeches Uncle Budrick.

A bolt of white light bursts from the tip of Millie's wand and rockets into the sky. From the ground, it looks like a flaming comet. But what good will THAT do?

"Greetings, young travelers!" a strange voice calls from the tangle of bushes behind us. We whirl around just as a ragged figure comes crashing into the clearing.

Wow. Don't ask me who this old guy is, but his timing is INCREDIBLE. The corpses are just a few paces away as he charges, swinging his sword over his head like a madman.

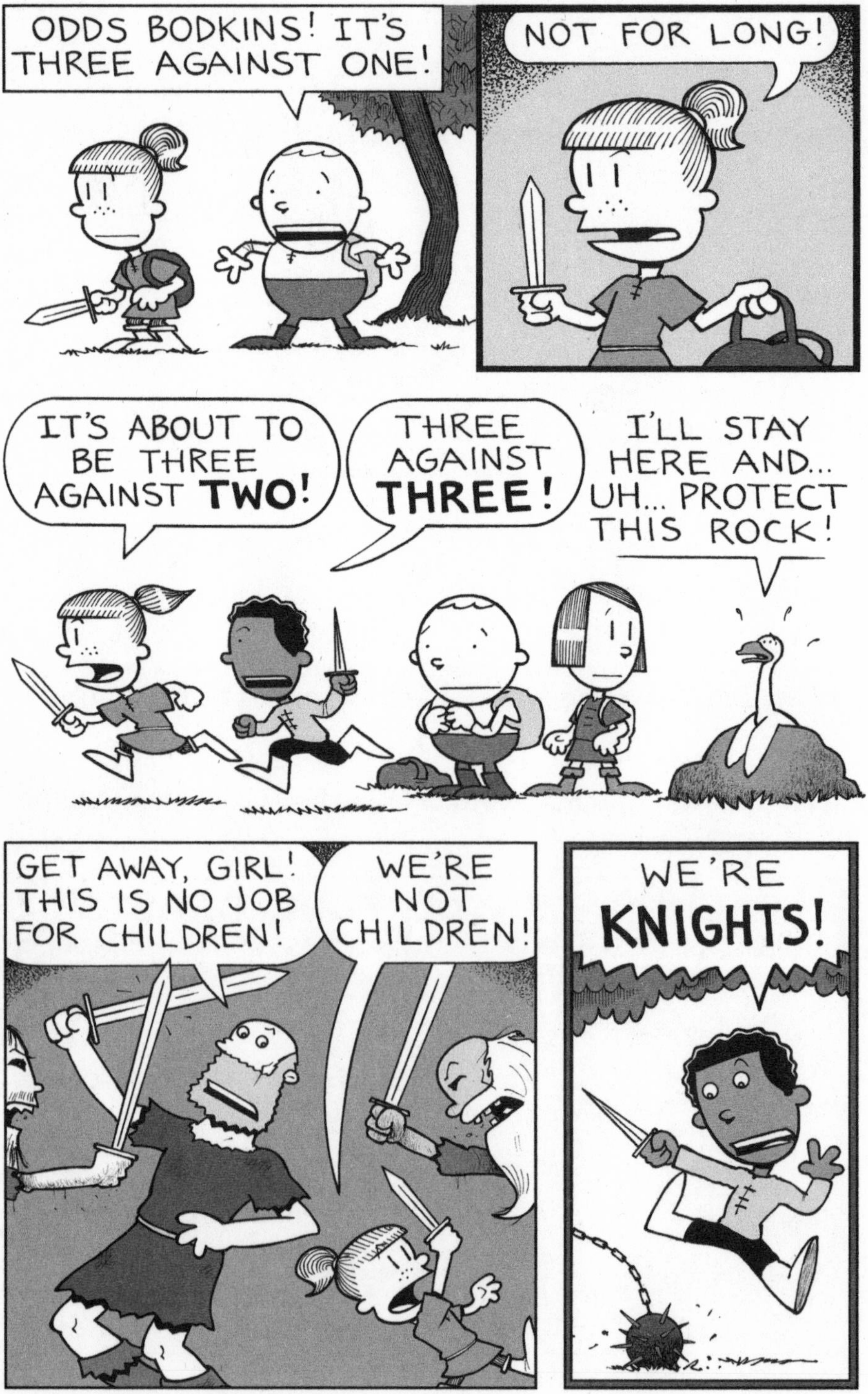
ODDS BODKINS! IT'S THREE AGAINST ONE!
NOT FOR LONG!
IT'S ABOUT TO BE THREE AGAINST **TWO**!
THREE AGAINST **THREE**!
I'LL STAY HERE AND... UH... PROTECT THIS ROCK!
GET AWAY, GIRL! THIS IS NO JOB FOR CHILDREN!
WE'RE NOT CHILDREN!
WE'RE **KNIGHTS!**

The battle rages on. Well, maybe "battle" isn't the right word. Simon and I are basically trying not to get killed. The stranger is doing most of the real work.

"We must force these monsters back beneath the earth!" he shouts over the clashing of weapons.

SOUNDS GREAT!

HOW?

SUNLIGHT IS THEIR WEAKNESS!

FOLLOW MY LEAD!

Twisting and lunging, the man drives one of the corpses away from the gravestones. With each swing of his sword, he's pushing the creature closer to a nearby patch of weeds. There, a shaft of light has found its way through the thick blanket of overhanging branches.

As the thing topples into the sunlight, it lets loose a hideous shriek. Rolling on the ground like it's on fire, it kicks its way into the safety of the shadows. Then all three creatures scramble frantically back toward the open graves.

What a relief. Not that I didn't enjoy our time with the three amigos, but the smell of rotting flesh was starting to bug me.

Kevyn bounces over to the old man, his face flushed with excitement. "Our sincerest thanks, my good fellow, for coming to our rescue!"

The stranger bows briefly. "It is my pleasure," he declares.

The old man nods at each of the others. Then his gaze falls on me. "You," he says. "Max."

There's sadness in his smile. "I once served the king."

"That was many years ago," Gadabout says.

"What's a knight doing in such a place?" Millie asks with a shiver. "It's . . . not very pleasant."

"I live here," Gadabout replies, his face turning grim. "But not by choice. As many have done, I took this road without understanding its true purpose."

Uncle Budrick gulps. "Wh-what IS its true purpose?"

"It's a tomb." He sighs. "All who walk this path must perish here. That's why it's called the Trail of the Dead."

I'M REALLY BEGINNING TO DESPISE THAT NAME.

BUT... CAN'T WE JUST GO BACK THE WAY WE CAME?

"No," Gadabout says. "The forest is bewitched. The trail disappears as soon as it's traveled. To retrace one's steps cannot be done."

I'M SORRY, MY FRIENDS.

THERE'S NO ESCAPE. YOU WILL LIVE OUT YOUR DAYS IN THESE HAUNTED WOODS.

"D-did you say haunted?" Kevyn gulps. "B-by whom?"

"By the dead," Gadabout answers. "They live below the ground, as you saw just now."

"But there has to be SOME way out of here!" I protest.

Gadabout shrugs. "A gateway exists. But there's no passing through it. It has been sealed for centuries."

And so we begin a long journey, following the old knight deeper into the forest. I see now why he called this place bewitched. As we walk, the trail vanishes behind us, swallowed up by a dark wall of vines and brambles.

We continue for several hours, until . . .

"It has the same markings on the handle as my DAGGER!"

He nods. "Indeed. Like your dagger, this sword once belonged to King Conrad."

"When the royal blades touch, an immense power is said to be unleashed," Gadabout explains.

"Immense enough for us to blast our way out of these woods?" Simon asks, gazing at the thick barrier of trees lining the trail.

Gadabout shakes his head. "We may not use them in such a way. The blades are destined for only one purpose."

> When one day from a lofty stage
> An evil monarch raves,
>
> When wicked magic in disguise
> Has turned free folk to slaves,
>
> When Death prepares to strike a blow,
> When hope seems all but lost,
>
> Then and only then may Conrad's
> Royal blades be crossed.

"How utterly fascinating!" Kevyn exclaims. "And a jolly good poem, too!"

"Tell us more about the king's sword, Sir Gadabout," Millie pleads as we resume our trek. "How did YOU end up with it?"

"That's right," Gadabout confirms.

 I WANDERED FOR MANY DAYS.

 THEN... !!! WHA-? IT'S NOT **POSSIBLE!**

I CAME TO A CLEARING, AND STANDING BEFORE ME WAS **KING CONRAD** HIMSELF!

"WAIT a minute!" I interrupt. "Conrad is DEAD!"

"Patience, Max," Kevyn tells me. "I suspect this tale is about to take an unexpected turn."

"Aye," Gadabout agrees. "It is."

 I RUSHED TO GREET THE KING, OVERJOYED.

 BUT SUDDENLY... POOF!

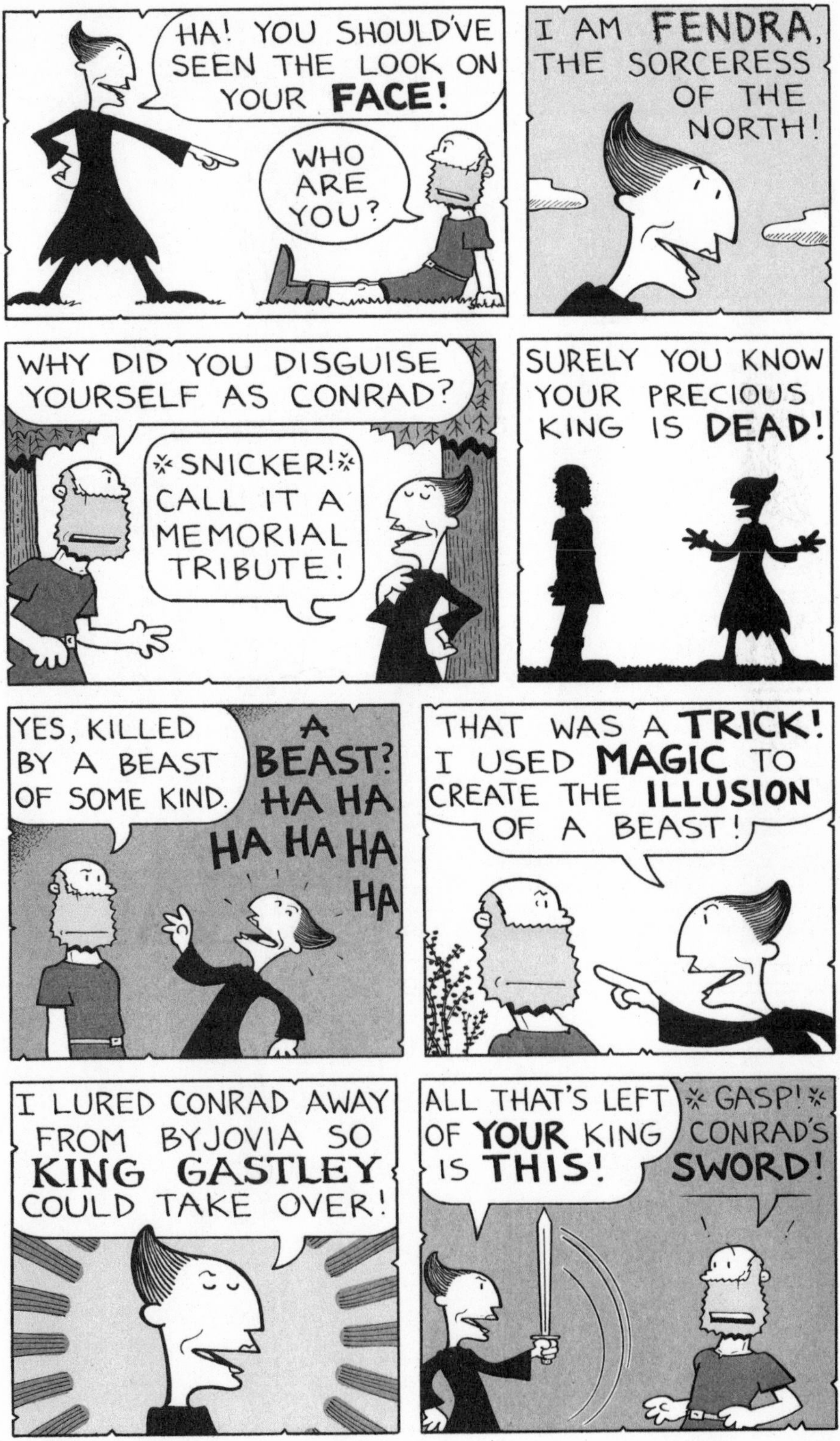
HA! YOU SHOULD'VE SEEN THE LOOK ON YOUR FACE!
WHO ARE YOU?
I AM FENDRA, THE SORCERESS OF THE NORTH!
WHY DID YOU DISGUISE YOURSELF AS CONRAD?
SNICKER! CALL IT A MEMORIAL TRIBUTE!
SURELY YOU KNOW YOUR PRECIOUS KING IS DEAD!
YES, KILLED BY A BEAST OF SOME KIND.
A BEAST? HA HA HA HA HA HA
THAT WAS A TRICK! I USED MAGIC TO CREATE THE ILLUSION OF A BEAST!
I LURED CONRAD AWAY FROM BYJOVIA SO KING GASTLEY COULD TAKE OVER!
ALL THAT'S LEFT OF YOUR KING IS THIS!
GASP! CONRAD'S SWORD!

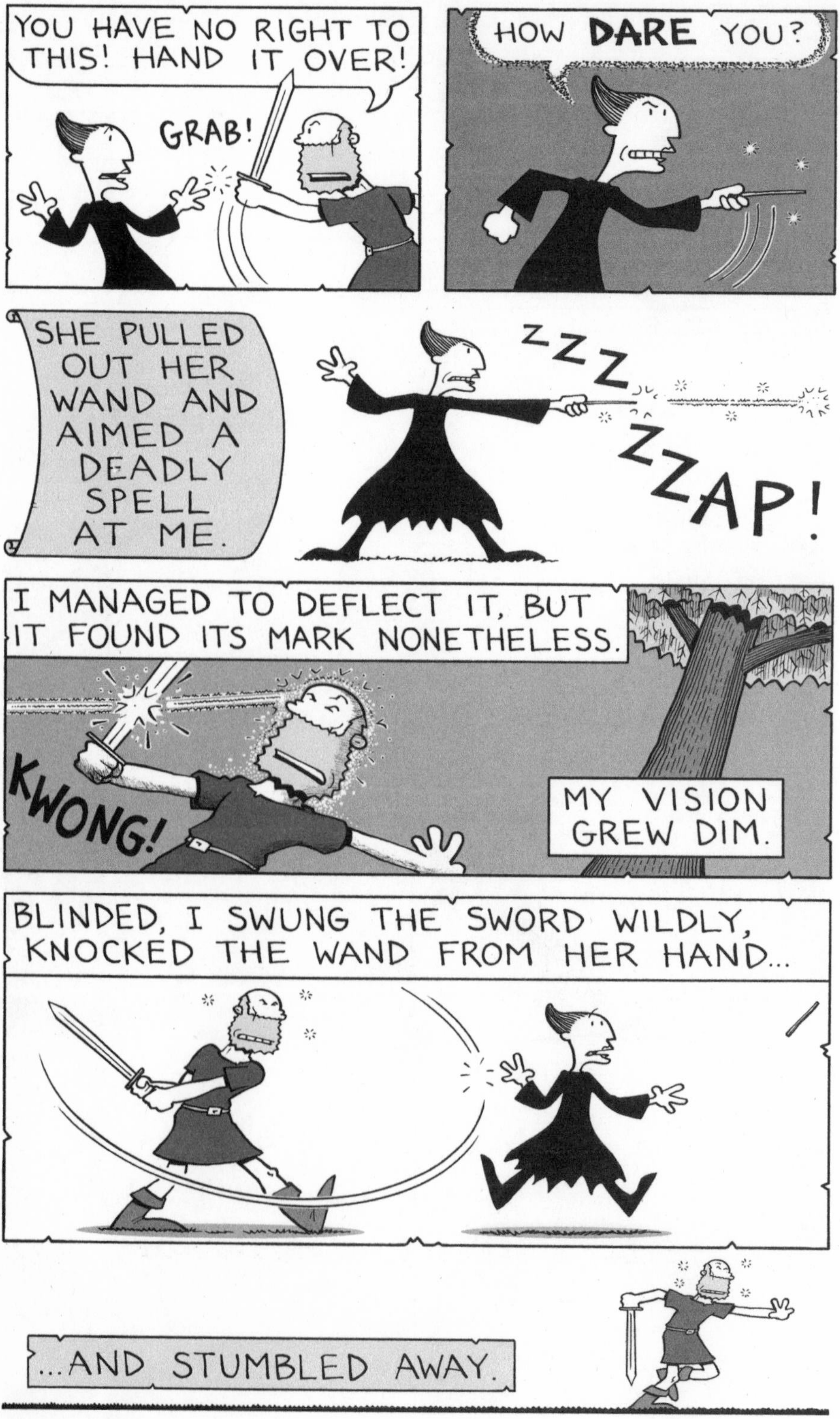
YOU HAVE NO RIGHT TO THIS! HAND IT OVER!
GRAB!
HOW DARE YOU?
SHE PULLED OUT HER WAND AND AIMED A DEADLY SPELL AT ME.
ZZZZZAP!
I MANAGED TO DEFLECT IT, BUT IT FOUND ITS MARK NONETHELESS.
KWONG!
MY VISION GREW DIM.
BLINDED, I SWUNG THE SWORD WILDLY, KNOCKED THE WAND FROM HER HAND...
...AND STUMBLED AWAY.

"So . . . you couldn't SEE?" I exclaim.

"I could not. The spell wore off after a few days, thank goodness, but by then it was too late. I'd already strayed onto the Trail of the Dead."

"It's HUGE," I say, staring up at the massive stone doors.

"Who built this thing?" Simon asks.

"I don't know," Gadabout answers. "The markings over the archway are unfamiliar to me. I cannot read them."

If thou wishest to go free,
A magic wand will be the key.

"All right," Millie says, taking the wand from her tunic. "I'm willing to give it a shot."

AHEM! ABRACADABRA.

OPEN SESAME.

BIPPITY BOPPITY BOO.

IT'S NOT BUDGING!

I SAY! **LOOK!**

THERE'S AN ODDLY SHAPED **HOLE** IN THE DOOR!

"A MAGIC WAND WILL BE THE KEY"! THE **KEY!** YOU SEE?

MILLIE! PUT THE WAND IN THAT SLOT!

The wand slides into the hole with a loud click, followed by a deep, creaking rumble. Then . . .

We rush through the doors, leaving the gloomy forest behind us and tumbling into an open field. It feels amazing to be out in the open air—especially for Gadabout.

We stretch out on the fragrant grass. Simon fashions a fishing pole and starts trying to catch us some dinner. Uncle Budrick and Millie fall asleep. I'm about to close my eyes, too, until Gadabout sits down beside me and Kevyn.

"You mentioned the Book of Prophecies," he begins.

WHERE DID YOU SEE IT? THOSE PAGES ARE THE DOMAIN OF **SORCERERS**!

QUITE RIGHT! IT WAS **MUMBLIN THE MAGICIAN** WHO SHARED IT WITH US!

The old man's eyes brighten. "Mumblin! He and I know each other well from our days with Conrad."

HE ONCE ACCIDENTALLY TURNED ME INTO A RASPBERRY SMOOTHIE!

"You think that's bad? He turned Uncle Budrick into a goose," I say.

Gadabout looks only mildly surprised. "Ah, so that's your UNCLE! When I saw that you had a talking goose with you . . ."

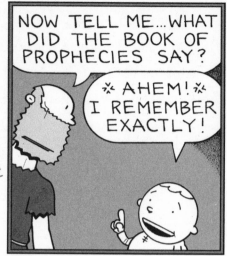

Kevyn recounts the passage about me saving Byjovia from Gastley. It's sort of embarrassing hearing words like "hero" and "rescuer" tossed around. I try not to listen. But Gadabout is hanging on every syllable.

"Good heavens, Max," he says. "For a small girl, you have a rather large task before you."

I do as he asks. Towering over me, Gadabout pulls Conrad's sword from his belt.

"Max," he proclaims. "By the power vested in me as commander of King Conrad's Royal Guard . . ."

...I HEREBY DECLARE YOU A KNIGHT OF THE REALM!

"What's the problem?" I ask.

"Well ... knights are always MALE," Gadabout answers, looking a bit sheepish. "I'm not certain how to address you."

I CAN'T VERY WELL CALL YOU **SIR** MAX, CAN I?

HEY, WHY **NOT**?

UNCLE BUDRICK CALLS HIMSELF "SIR," AND HE'S ONLY A **TROUBADOUR!**

⁂AHEM!⁂ DID YOU SAY **ONLY** A TROUBADOUR?

Whoops. I didn't know he was listening. Looks like I might have ruffled a few feathers.

UH... WHAT I MEANT WAS... UMM...

IT'S ALL RIGHT, MAX. I GET IT.

I'VE KNOWN FOR A WHILE NOW THAT YOU DON'T WANT TO BE AN ENTERTAINER.

I can hardly believe my ears. "You HAVE?"

"It's sort of obvious," he tells me. "As we say in the troubadour biz, you're musically challenged."

Yeah, I know what you're thinking: girls CAN'T be knights. But I'm choosing to ignore that little fact. If Sir Gadabout himself thinks I'm up for the job . . .

FYI: It's not a mobile. Simon caught enough brook trout to make a proper feast. Millie and I collect some wood and build a roaring campfire. An hour later, we've all eaten our fill.

"By accident, I guess you'd say," Millie begins. "I grew up in a Byjovian orphanage."

"I see," Gadabout murmurs, scratching his beard.

By the firelight, I can see Simon's eyes turn misty. "No," he sniffs. "I had parents."

"Had?" Kevyn clears his throat. "Are they . . . dead?"

Gadabout leans forward intently. "How so?"

"They became coldhearted," Simon continues. "It was like they were in a trance. They stopped caring for me."

"I spent less and less time at home," he explains.

Wow. And I thought MY life was tough. Poor Simon. I wonder what made his parents act like that.

Gadabout has a theory:

He nods, his face frowning. "People's hearts and minds don't change so completely without a reason."

"AHA!" Uncle Budrick honks.

"You're quite right, Max," Gadabout says. "Children are generally immune to the effects of wicked magic."

"What about Kevyn's parents?" Millie points out.

"... but Mumblin once told me that people react to magical spells as to a pox. Most are infected. A few are not."

"In other words," Kevyn declares, "my parents were lucky."

Gadabout gazes up at the evening sky. "The moon is bright, and there are no clouds to speak of. We will have fine weather for traveling tomorrow, I think."

"We?" I repeat.

The old man smiles as he stretches out on the ground. "Sometimes those are the best kinds of journeys."

The next morning, we resume our trek. It's fun having Gadabout along. He tells us about his adventures with Conrad back in the day. And when he runs out of stories, Uncle Budrick is happy to pick up the slack.

"That plant was booby-trapped!" Simon gasps.

We rush over. The old knight's eyes are open. He's alive.

But he's not moving. And when he speaks, his voice is faint.

"I'll try it," Millie says. She waves it over his body, tracing circles through the air. Nothing happens. I place a hand on his chest. I can barely feel a heartbeat.

I kneel beside Gadabout, holding the ring Mumblin gave me the night we left. I'm not sure if a washed-up wizard can save his life, but I know WE can't. His skin is turning pale. His breathing is raspy.

"You're going to see an old friend," I tell him, and he manages a weak smile. There's a lump in my throat. Come on, Max, hold it together. Knights don't cry.

I lift Gadabout's arm off the floor. It's deadweight in my hands. I slide the ring onto his finger. Then, with a gentle push, I force it past the knuckles.

If levitating means rising off the floor . . . then yeah, that's what's happening. An instant later, Gadabout's whole body is bathed in a shimmering light. Then . . .

He vanishes.

YOU'RE STILL A **BEGINNER!** EVENTUALLY, YOU'LL **LEARN** HOW TO BE A GREAT MAGICIAN!

BUT LEARNING TAKES **TIME!** IT TAKES **PATIENCE!** IT TAKES...

...**BOOKS!**

! !

LOOK AT 'EM ALL!

IT'S A VERITABLE **LIBRARY!**

"CONJURING FOR DUMMIES."

"BEWITCHING BREWS."

"HOW TO JINX FRIENDS AND INFLUENCE PEOPLE."

"SPELLS A-POPPIN.'"

THEY'RE ALL ABOUT WIZARDRY!

THIS IS THE HOUSE OF A **MAGICIAN!**

NOT JUST **ANY MAGICIAN!**

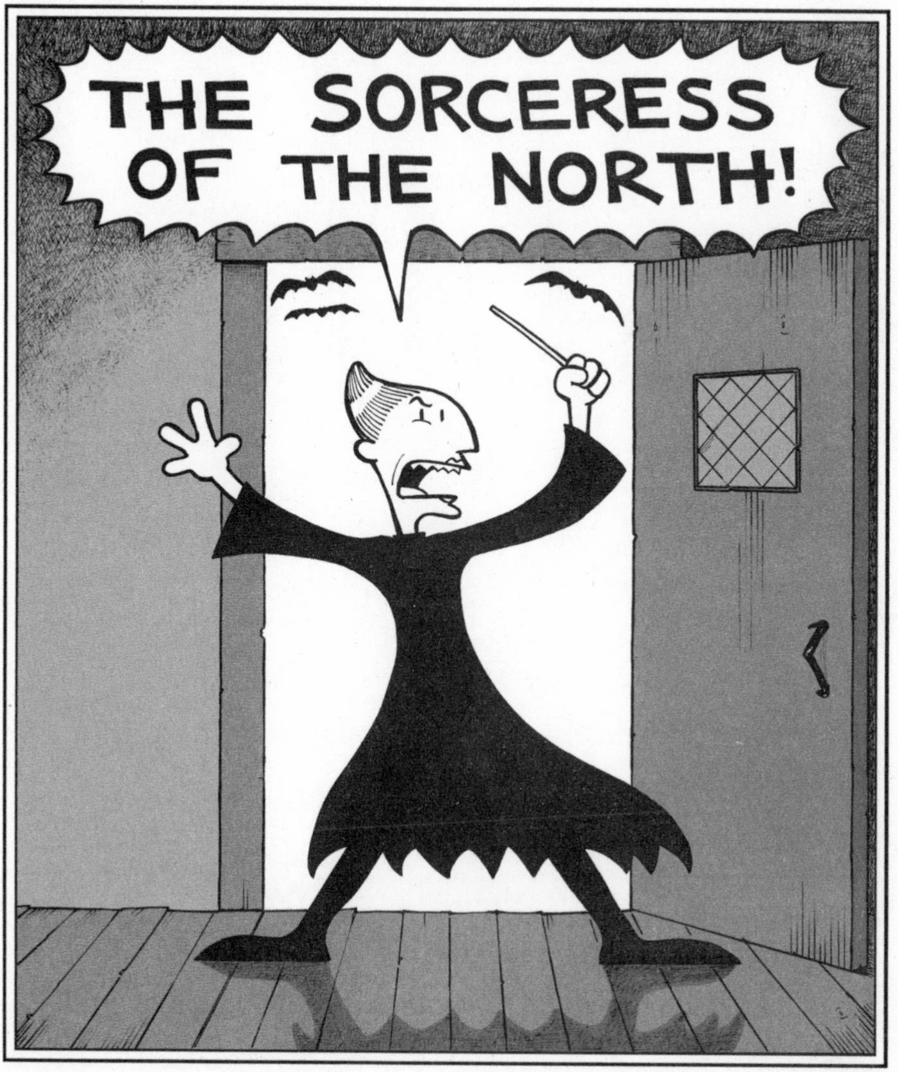
THE SORCERESS OF THE NORTH!

11

I've gotta hand it to her: she knows how to make an entrance.

"You're Fendra," I say. Not the most brilliant observation, I'll admit, but I didn't have anything clever prepared.

"What makes you so sure?" I ask her, trying to sound extra knightly.

YOU WEREN'T THERE!

She smirks. "King Gastley and I are close, girlie. He told me all about your little visit to the throne room."

NOW SAY YOUR GOODBYES!

I'M ABOUT TO **DO AWAY WITH YOU!**

Simon takes a step toward her. "No, you're not. You CAN'T."

GADABOUT SAYS CHILDREN AREN'T **AFFECTED** BY DARK MAGIC.

Fendra pauses. For the briefest of moments, she looks surprised. But she recovers quickly.

"Yes, there are some rather annoying protections in place where children are concerned," she concedes icily. "But trust me, I am still capable of doing you immense harm."

Millie's got her wand out, and she's taking dead aim at Fendra's heart. Her voice shakes, but her hand is steady.

Fendra stares in astonishment. Then she unleashes a gale of mocking laughter. "Oh, this is PRICELESS!"

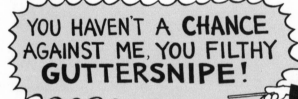

Okay, that guttersnipe comment was totally obnoxious, but Fendra might have a point. Millie just got through telling us she's not a real magician yet.

How can she compete with a world-class witch who has a whole KINGDOM under her thumb?

Answer: she can't.

"You're out of your depth, dearie," Fendra cackles.

Millie crumples against the bookcase. Fendra pivots toward the rest of us, twirling the wand between her clawlike fingers. Without thinking, I reach for the dagger at my hip.

Fendra takes a step back—not in fear, but in surprise. She's staring at the blade in my hand, and it's clear from the eager glint in her eyes that she's seen it before.

"You've just made me rethink this situation, girl," she says, inching closer. "At first, I was angry that you'd broken into my house . . . but now, I see you've brought me a GIFT."

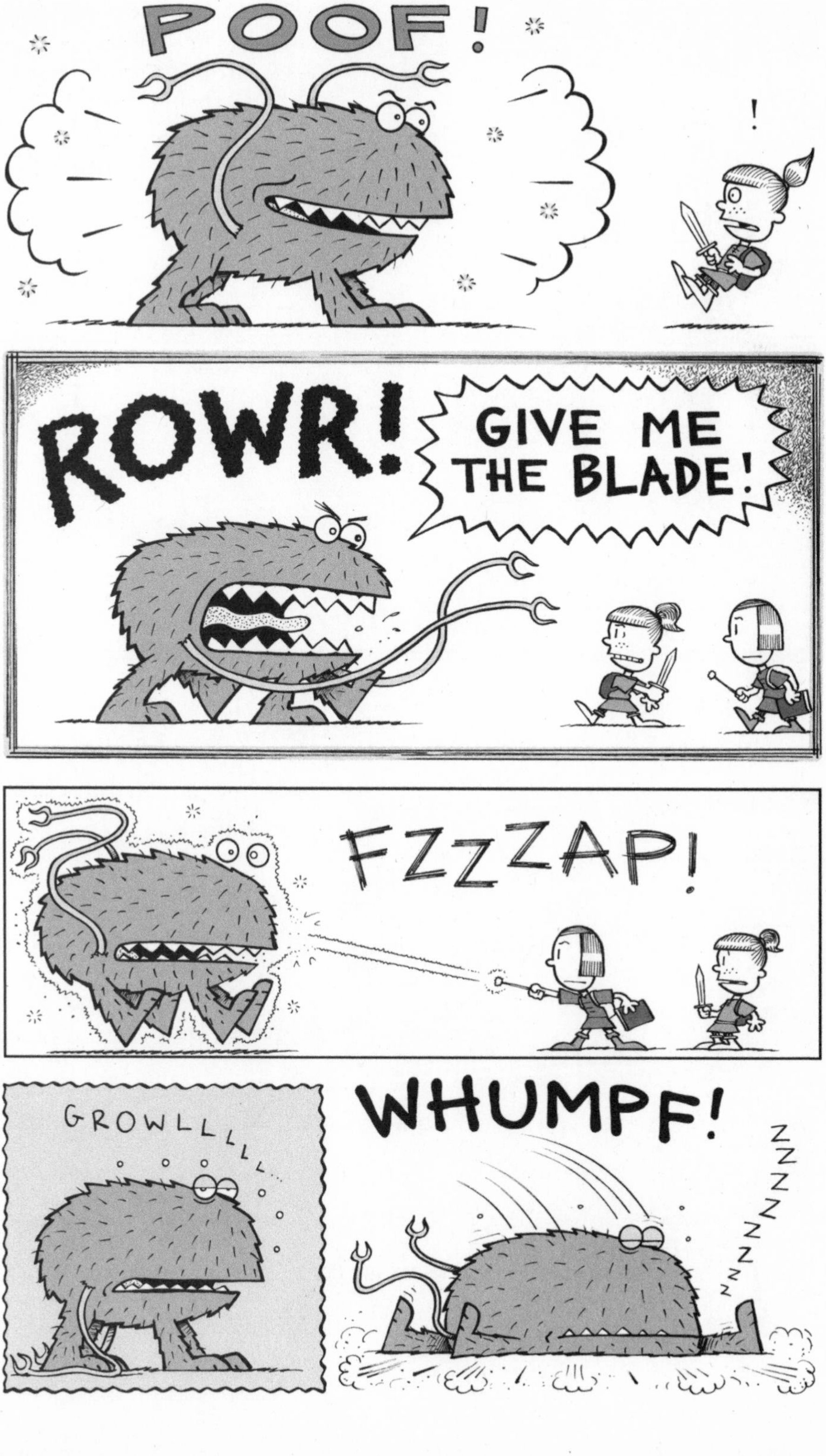
POOF!
!
ROWR!
GIVE ME THE BLADE!
FZZZAP!
GROWLLLLL...
WHUMPF!
ZZZZZZZZ

"I propose we take that book with us, Millie," Kevyn says. "It may come in handy."

"I agree," she answers. "And I think we should get away from here as quickly as possible. Spells cast by beginning magicians don't last very long."

"I thought geese had a built-in sense of direction," says Simon. "You know, for migrating and whatnot."

"You seem to have forgotten that I'm not a real goose," Uncle Budrick grouses. "I'm a TROUBADOUR!"

...AND I'M READY TO BE A **PERSON** AGAIN!

"The next time we see Mumblin, ask him to change you back," Simon suggests.

"Are you serious? You've seen the man try to do magic!" Uncle Budrick squawks. "He's a DISASTER!"

Before long, we've left Fendra's house far behind us. The others chat as we trudge along, but I don't feel like talking. My brain's too full of questions about this adventure.

I get no answers—which isn't a surprise, by the way. I'm not expecting some mysterious voice to tell me what to do.

"Ah! Max! How goes the journey?" Mumblin chirps, as if speaking through a banana is an everyday occurrence.

"Not too bad," I answer. "Um . . . so this banana is just like your magic grapefruit, huh?"

"Don't be absurd, my dear girl. . . ."

"Yes, I took him to Alice and Nolan's house, and we're nursing him back to health. He's going to be fine."

Mumblin's voice crackles and fades into silence. I shake the banana, hoping to somehow restore the connection. But I guess I shake it too hard. It breaks apart in my hand.

"At least Mumblin was able to let us know Sir Gadabout's okay," Millie points out.

"Yes, but he was also attempting to convey a warning," Kevyn reminds us. "There is danger ahead."

I set the dagger on a flat piece of ground and spin it. Sure enough, it comes to a stop with the tip facing the hills that rise in the distance.

"True north," I announce. "Let's keep going, Midknights."

We hike for several days, eating the few handfuls of berries we find along the route. The fields and forests give way to rugged foothills and scattered boulders. Eventually, we find ourselves at the base of a cold gray mountain.

PLEASE TELL ME WE'RE NOT CLIMBING THAT!

"I don't think we'll have to," Kevyn says.

LOOK THERE! IT APPEARS TO BE A **TUNNEL**!

WE'LL GO **UNDER** THE MOUNTAIN, NOT OVER IT!

Simon pulls a bundle of dry sticks from his sack. "I collected these for firewood," he says. "But they'll work well as torches."

Moments later, we step into a world darker than the inky waters of Gastley's moat. The torches provide some dim light, but only enough to cast eerie shadows on the cavern walls. We move slowly, feeling our way forward. Hours crawl by.

"I hesitate to say this," Kevyn whispers, "but what will we do when our torches expire?"

Millie's right. There's a screech—faint at first, but growing louder as we follow the tunnel's sloping passageway.

The tunnel expands into a giant vault. Far below us, dozens of grimy figures bite and claw at each other. They stand on two feet like people, but they're not human. They're covered with slick hair, and as they scuffle around a smoldering fire, they gnash their jagged rows of yellow teeth.

They've stopped fighting. I hear a chorus of snorts and sniffs as the rats point their noses toward our hiding spot. Then, without warning, several of them leap off the ground with a few flaps of their leathery wings. They're coming for us.

They snatch us up like crumbs and carry us through the darkness. Then we're dropped with a thud on the cavern floor.

We scramble to our feet, but they've already formed a tight circle around us. We're trapped.

We've lost our torches, so we huddle close to the rats' dying fire. The ground trembles. The thunderous noise grows louder.

There—on the far side of the cavern. Did something just move? Peering through the murk that fills the chamber, I see a shadow, huge and black. We hear the harsh echo of claws scraping against stone.

"Whatever it is, it's too big to be a rat," Simon whispers.
I nod in agreement. "That's no rat."

I've never seen a dragon before. Uncle Budrick's told me plenty of stories about them, but I always figured he was just blowing smoke. I didn't actually think dragons were REAL.

Maybe it wasn't the rats Mumblin was warning me about. It might have been THIS guy. He looks primed to chew me to bits and use King Conrad's dagger as a toothpick.

Which reminds me: I should probably try to defend myself. After all, I'm a knight of the realm. Slaying dragons is part of the job. I pull the dagger from my belt, point it straight at him, and try to think of something gallant to say.

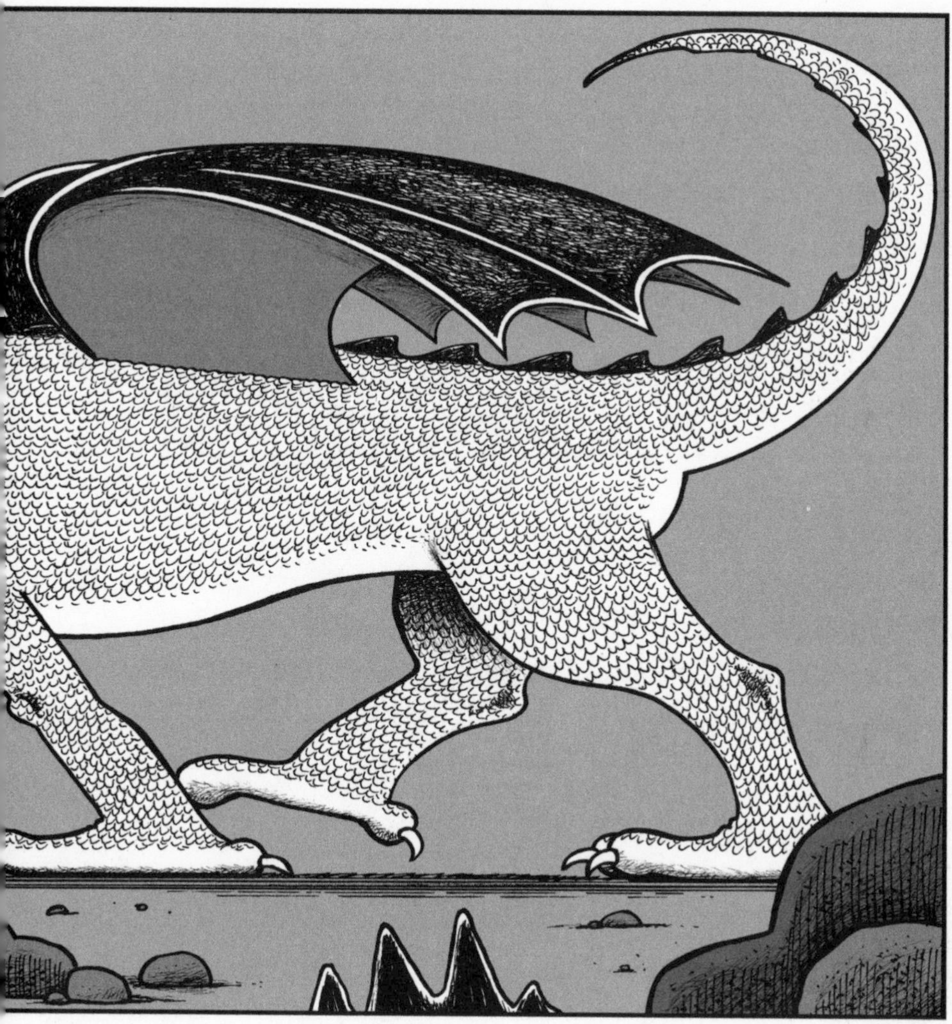

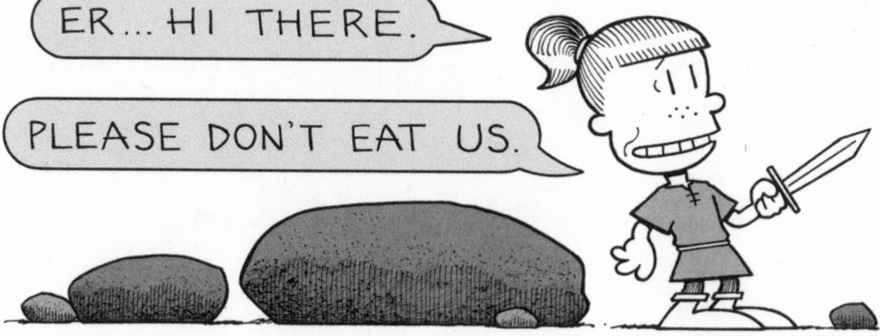
ER... HI THERE.
PLEASE DON'T EAT US.

And guess what? It WORKS! At least that's what it seems like at first. The dragon hesitates, and his orange eyes soften. But a second later, I realize it's not me he's looking at. And it's nothing I've said that makes him stop in his tracks.

It's the DAGGER!

It's no secret there's something special about it. Gadabout told me so back on the Trail of the Dead. But it's never acted like THIS before. Suddenly it feels  featherlight. The handle is tingling, sending a warm buzz up the length of my arm. And a bright blue halo hovers around the blade.

The dragon lowers his head to the cavern floor.

"Royal blades have special powers," Kevyn reminds us. "Possessing Conrad's dagger undoubtedly makes this dragon yours to command!"

"Great," I say. "What am I supposed to do with a dragon?"

"Climb on his back, that's what!" Simon shouts.

Holy smoke. I had no idea breathing fire was such a useful skill. When the dust clears, we can see a stretch of blue sky beyond the brand-new passageway. A welcome blast of cold air tickles my face. I feel the dragon's muscles tense as he settles into a crouch and unfolds his wings. Prepare for liftoff.

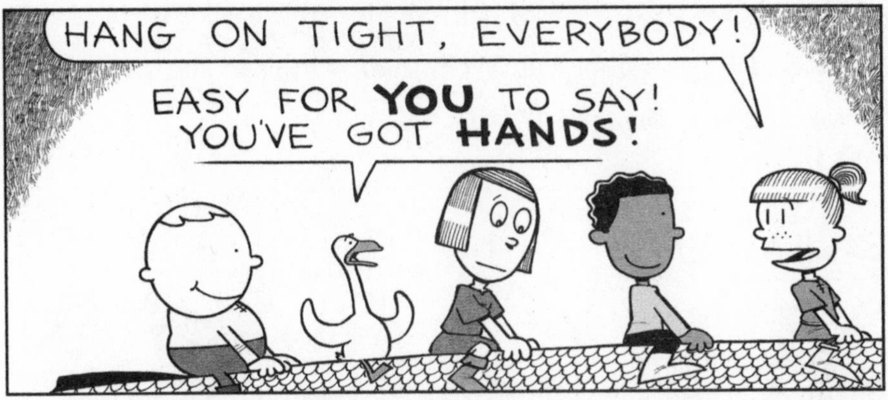
HANG ON TIGHT, EVERYBODY!
EASY FOR **YOU** TO SAY! YOU'VE GOT **HANDS**!

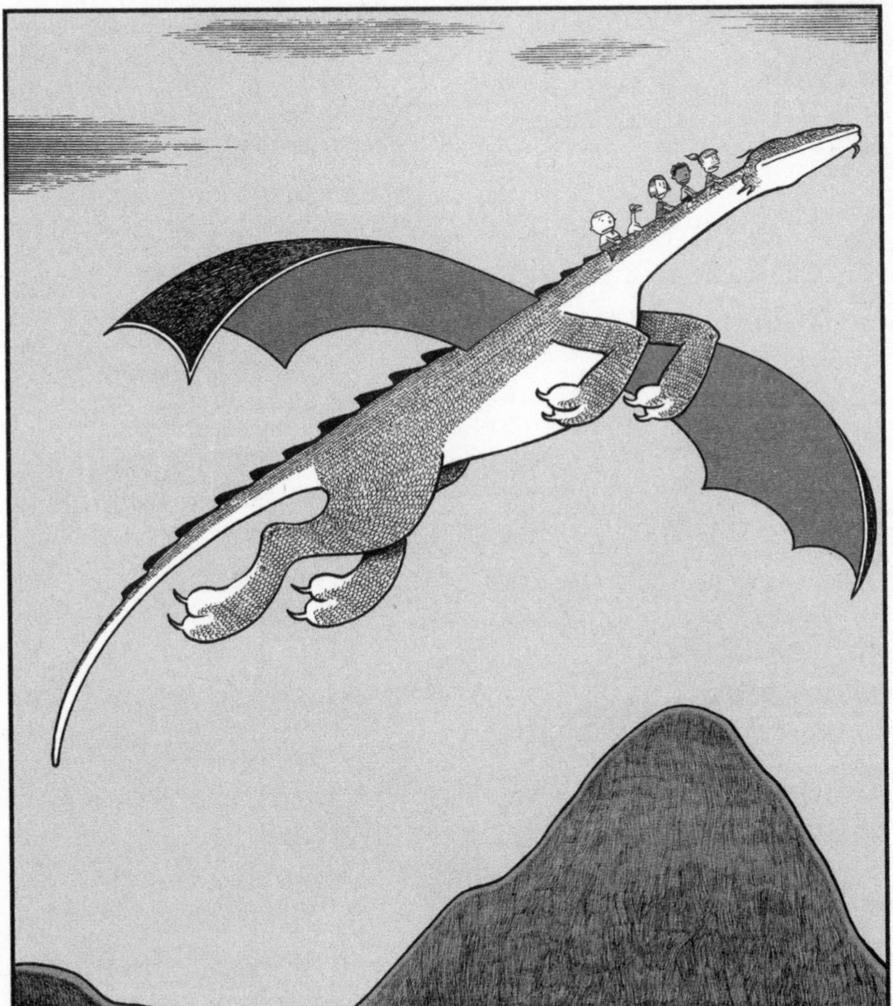

We rocket up and away from the mountain like we've been launched from a catapult. We're half a mile in the air before I can catch my breath.

"Flamethrower!" Kevyn proposes.

"Giantwings!" I suggest.

"How about Bruce?" Millie says.

"Where's he taking us?" I wonder.

"Somewhere far away," Simon guesses. "Maybe even to the edge of the earth."

"Some say the earth HAS no edges," Kevyn declares.

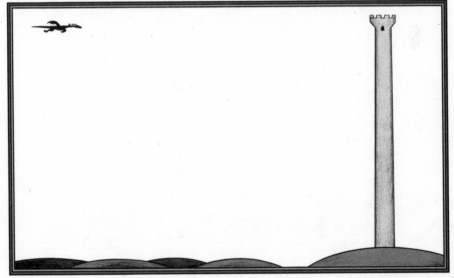

Below us, we see a series of squatty hills. Atop the largest of them, like a single stalk of wheat rising from a dirt mound, sits a humongous marble tower. It's not attached to any

castle or surrounded by a city. It stands alone. And judging by the way Bruce has begun a slow descent, that tower is right where we're headed. Moments later, we're on the ground, staring up at the enormous column.

"Do you suppose someone LIVES here?" Millie asks.

Simon runs his hand against the wall. "It might not be for living in. It could be just a statue."

"If that's true," Kevyn says, noticing a small opening near the top of the turret . . .

...WHY DOES IT HAVE A **WINDOW?**

"And if there's a WINDOW," Simon adds, circling the base of the tower, "shouldn't there be a DOOR?"

We fall silent, listening. There it is again: a tiny voice floating down from the very top of the tower.

"That sounds like a kid," Millie says.

Simon nods. "A kid who's TRAPPED in there."

"My fellow Midknights!" Kevyn cries. "Our duty is clear!"

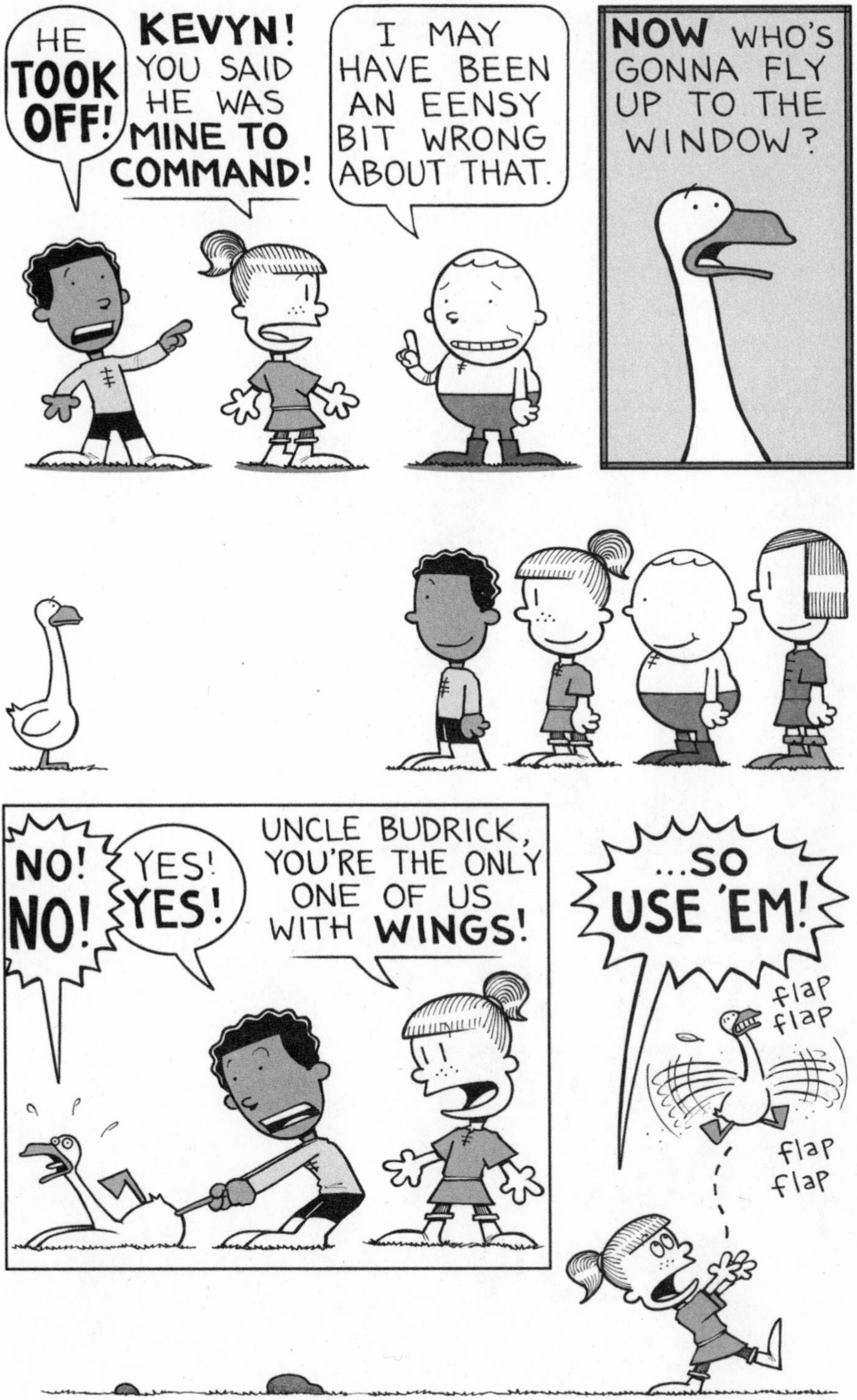
HE TOOK OFF!
KEVYN! YOU SAID HE WAS MINE TO COMMAND!
I MAY HAVE BEEN AN EENSY BIT WRONG ABOUT THAT.
NOW WHO'S GONNA FLY UP TO THE WINDOW?
NO! NO!
YES! YES!
UNCLE BUDRICK, YOU'RE THE ONLY ONE OF US WITH WINGS!
...SO USE 'EM!
flap flap
flap flap

Sometimes it's good to have a goose in the family. He's not a GRACEFUL goose, mind you, but Uncle Budrick gets the job done. He flails and flaps his way to the top of the tower and slips through the window. Down below, we wait.

"I beg your pardon if this sounds overly pessimistic," Kevyn says after a long pause.

...BUT IS YOUR UNCLE STRONG ENOUGH TO CARRY SOMEONE FROM THE TOP OF THE TOWER TO THE GROUND?

HEADS UP!

COMIN' THROUGH! LOOK OUT BELOW!

The kid sits up. He's a boy, with short hair, sky-blue eyes, and kind of a round face. For just a second, I feel a brief stab of recognition, as if I've met him before. But that's impossible. I shake it off and help him to his feet.

"Perhaps he was injured during his fall," Kevyn says. "A blow to the head can affect one's memory."

"But he acted the same way when I found him in the tower," Uncle Budrick points out. "He had no idea how he got there."

The boy looks pained. "I have asked myself all those questions, but I can find no answers. What I DO know is that I've lived in this tower for a very long time."

I'VE COUNTED **TWO THOUSAND SUNSETS** FROM MY WINDOW.

Millie gasps. "That's over FIVE YEARS!"

"So you were just a LITTLE guy when you got locked up!" I say.

He scratches his head. "I don't know what you mean. I was no smaller then than I am today."

HUH? YOU HAVEN'T **GROWN?**

GROWN? NO.

FASCINATING!

FANTASTIC!

FREAKY.

"Now wait a minute," Simon insists. "What about FOOD? If you haven't left that tower for five years, how come you haven't starved to death?"

"The woman brings me food."

"What woman?" we all ask together.

The boy shrugs. "I don't know what to call her."

He kneels and begins making lines in the dust. A profile slowly forms: a sharp nose, upswept hair, and two beady eyes. It doesn't take magic to recognize THAT face.

"I should have known she was behind this," I growl.

The boy's confused. "Who is Fendra?"

"She is a most disagreeable sorceress," Kevyn answers. "And unless I am sorely mistaken . . ."

"This young fella must be IMPORTANT in some way," Uncle Budrick says, waving a wing at our new friend.

Millie brings out the book she found at Fendra's house and begins searching the pages. "Aha!" she says after a few moments. "There's something here called an Amnesia Curse."

He nods. "I'd like to know how it feels to remember."

The boy staggers, shaking his head and blinking hard. Finally, he steadies himself, gazing first at us and then at the tower that looms over the rocky hilltop. His expression changes. The doubt and confusion slip away from his face.

"Well? Did it work?" Simon asks, sounding as impatient as we all feel. "Do you know who you are?"

The boy smiles, his eyes shining. "I do."

Wow, talk about DRAMA. All we can do is stare at him in wonder. It's a moment of complete stillness and—

"He disappeared five years ago," Kevyn explains. "People understandably assumed the worst."

The boy looks distressed. "But I'm alive! And I promise you, I AM the king!"

Sorry, I'm not buying it. What if this is another one of Fendra's underhanded tricks? If there's some sort of wicked magic at work here . . .

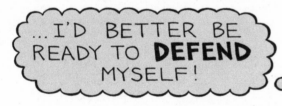

I draw the blade, hoping the boy won't notice. But he spots it. He jumps back, his face bright with excitement. "You have my dagger!" he cries.

I can't hide my surprise. "Wha—? How'd you—?"

"If a man owns a thing, and cares for it all his life," he says . . .

"The dagger will reveal who I am. Place it on the ground . . ."

He seems so certain, I'm starting to believe this kid really IS Conrad. I reach down, twirl the blade . . .

. . . and watch it spin to a stop at the boy's feet.

He smiles. "Make sure. Try again."

I spin it a second time. Then a third. Each attempt ends the same way: with the tip pointing directly at . . .

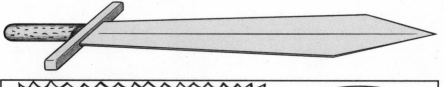

I hand him the dagger. "This belongs to you," I say. I don't know if I'm supposed to curtsy or bow or anything. I've never met a real king before. Gastley doesn't count.

He shakes my hand. "Thank you . . . uh . . ."

"Max," I tell him.

Kevyn corrects me. "SIR Max!"

SHE WAS **KNIGHTED** BY YOUR MAN **GADABOUT!**

Conrad's eyebrows arch skyward. "Now THAT sounds like a story worth hearing!"

PLEASE, ALL OF YOU: TELL ME WHO YOU ARE AND HOW YOU CAME TO BE HERE.

We introduce ourselves and describe everything that's happened since we left Byjovia.

"Great Scott!" Conrad exclaims. "That's quite a journey!"

YEAH, BUT WE HAD NO IDEA IT WOULD LEAD US TO **YOU!**

PERHAPS WE **SHOULD** HAVE! I'VE JUST REALIZED THE BOOK OF PROPHECIES **FORESAW** THIS!

"It was SHE who turned me into a child."

"But why?" Simon asks.

"To help my poor, misguided brother seize the throne," Conrad answers. "Listen to my tale, friends, and I believe the depths of their treachery will become clear."

AS YOU KNOW, I LEFT BYJOVIA IN SEARCH OF A MYSTERIOUS MONSTER...

I SAW TELLTALE SIGNS—RUINED COTTAGES AND CROPS BURNING IN THE FIELDS.

BUT WHEN I ASKED WHAT HAD HAPPENED, NO TWO STORIES MATCHED...

IT WAS A DRAGON.

IT WAS A BUNNY.

...AND THE PEOPLE ALL WORE THE SAME VACANT EXPRESSION.

HAD THERE **REALLY** BEEN A MONSTER?....

...OR HAD THESE POOR SOULS BEEN **BEWITCHED?** MY SUSPICIONS GREW.

I DECIDED TO RETURN TO BYJOVIA. BUT THEN...

HELP ME, KIND SIR!

I'VE BEEN BITTEN BY A DEADLY **SNAKE!**

ITS FANG IS STUCK IN MY LEG! PLEASE! LEND ME A BLADE SO I CAN CUT IT OUT!

I HANDED THE POOR FELLOW MY DAGGER, AND...

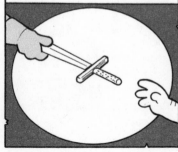

Millie breaks in. "Why did Gastley want your dagger?"

"He craves anything that will make him stronger," Conrad explains. "The dagger has immense power—especially when it is crossed with the sword."

"But YOU still had the sword," I remind him. "Couldn't you have used it to defeat him? Y'know, in a duel?"

The king nods. "Yes, I believe that I could have—if he'd faced me alone. But cowards seldom fight their own battles."

A DOZEN OF GASTLEY'S SOLDIERS JUST HAPPENED TO BE LURKING NEARBY.

GET HIM, GUYS!

I FOUGHT MY HARDEST, BUT I WAS OUTNUMBERED.

CLONG!

KLANG!

I WAS CERTAIN I'D BE KILLED...

...WHICH WAS CLEARLY WHAT MY BROTHER HAD IN MIND.

YES! YES! FINISH HIM OFF!

NO!!

WE NEED HIM **ALIVE**, YOU SIMPLETON!

BUT **ALIVE**, HE'S A **THREAT**!

NOT FOR **LONG**!

GASTLEY'S MEN STRIPPED ME OF MY ARMOR.

WATCH **THIS**!

ZZWIP!

THE **FORMER** KING IS NOW A HARMLESS **PIPSQUEAK**!

HA! SERVES HIM RIGHT!

! ! !

WELL, **LITTLE** BROTHER, YOU WON'T BE NEEDING YOUR **SWORD** ANYMORE!

BRING ME HIS **DAGGER**, PEASANT!

I WANT TO TRY THAT COOL "CROSSED BLADES" THING!

"That stranger is the guy who ROBBED us!" Uncle Budrick squawks. "So THAT's how he ended up with the dagger!"

"Gadzooks!" Kevyn exclaims. "Quite unintentionally, that thief provided a valuable service!"

"You're right," Conrad confirms. "He prevented my brother from possessing both royal blades."

"That's how it happened," Conrad concludes. "I've been a captive in the tower ever since."

Simon frowns. "There's one thing I don't understand. Why did Fendra insist on keeping you alive?"

Millie looks through her book of magic. "I've found the enchantment that Fendra is using to control the people of Byjovia," she says excitedly. "And Conrad's blood is the key ingredient!"

"A dragon's scale, An ogre's tooth, A pinch of Graveyard mud...  A serpent's skin, A spider's web, **A drop of Royal blood.**"

"It says here the blood must be fresh," Millie goes on. "And the enchantment lasts for one week."

"Egad! It all makes sense!" Kevyn cries. "Fendra has to renew the enchantment each week!"

THAT'S WHY SHE COLLECTS YOUR BLOOD EVERY SEVEN DAYS!

UH-OH.

WHAT?

TODAY'S THE SEVENTH DAY! FENDRA COULD ARRIVE ANY SECOND!

"We escaped from her once," Simon declares. "It might be pushing our luck to try it a second time."

WE NEED TO LEAVE. **NOW**.

TOO BAD BRUCE TOOK OFF.

IT WOULD BE FASTER TO **RIDE** INSTEAD OF WALK.

I SAY! WHY DON'T WE AVAIL OURSELVES OF THAT **HORSE**?

HORSE?

DUSTY!!

✳CHUCKLE!✳ THAT'S WHAT WE AUTHORS CALL A **PLOT TWIST**!

Kevyn shakes his head. "Max, all six of us can't possibly fit on Dusty. We need another horse."

Conrad takes one last glance at the lonely tower. "I thought that room would be my prison forever," he says. "Thank you, my friends, for my freedom . . . and my memory."

"Don't thank us yet," I tell him. "None of this means anything as long as Gastley's on the throne."

"Then we must ride south," Conrad announces.

"Your uncle certainly knows a lot of songs, Max," Conrad says.

We've stopped to rest after hours of riding, and Uncle Budrick has been serenading us every step of the way.

He's currently seventeen verses into "The Ballad of the Flatulent Tinsmith."

"Sorry about that," I whisper. "He loves to perform, and we're the only audience he has."

Conrad gives me a pat on the shoulder. "Take heart, my friend. Once we straighten out this mess in Byjovia . . ."

"Um . . . yeah, I'm sure HE will," I say, choosing my words carefully. "But personally, I'd rather do . . . something else."

"Surely you know that in Byjovia, girls cannot be knights."

He's the king. If anyone's going to have an answer, HE will.

"What if YOU couldn't be king just because you're a BOY? Would THAT be fair?"

Conrad seems a bit flustered. "I'll ... I'll admit it hadn't occurred to me that girls might—"

"It's not only GIRLS, Your Highness!" Kevyn cuts in.

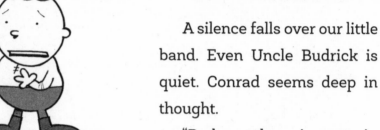

A silence falls over our little band. Even Uncle Budrick is quiet. Conrad seems deep in thought.

"Perhaps there is more in Byjovia that needs changing than I realized," he says finally, rising to his feet. "Thank you for your honesty, my friends. You've opened my eyes."

We hurry into a grove of nearby trees and crouch silently in the shadows. "What are we hiding from?" whispers Millie.

The Sorceress of the North is no longer the hairy creature we last saw snoring in her cabin. She's herself again, darting across the sky like a giant bat.

"She's undoubtedly just made her weekly visit to the Forgotten Tower," Kevyn murmurs.

"And learned that the blood bank is closed." Conrad grins.

"She's on her way to Byjovia," Conrad says, climbing onto Uncle Budrick. "By broomstick, she'll be there in a few hours."

None of us knows what a bus is, but Uncle Budrick doesn't care. He's on a roll. And so are we, covering mile after mile as the air grows warmer and the landscape more familiar. Finally, on the fifth day, we reach the crest of a hill. There it is below us:

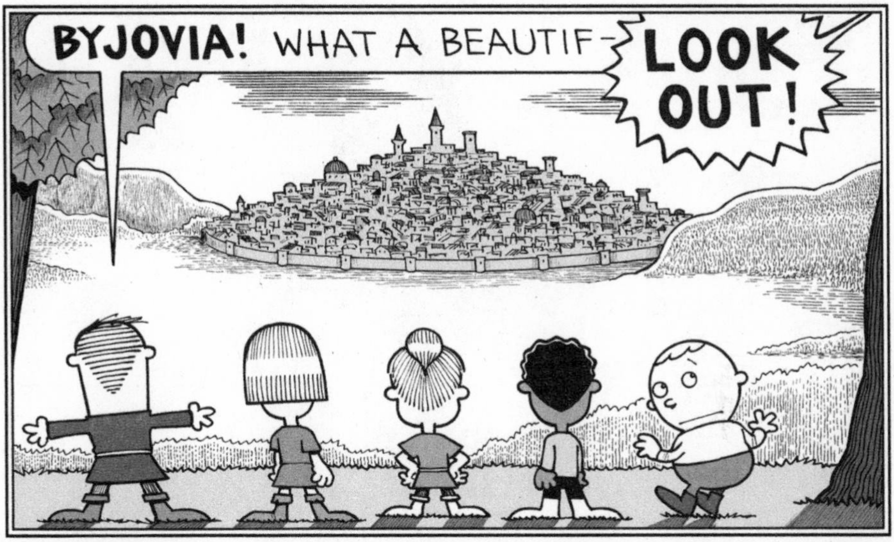
BYJOVIA! WHAT A BEAUTIF-
LOOK OUT!

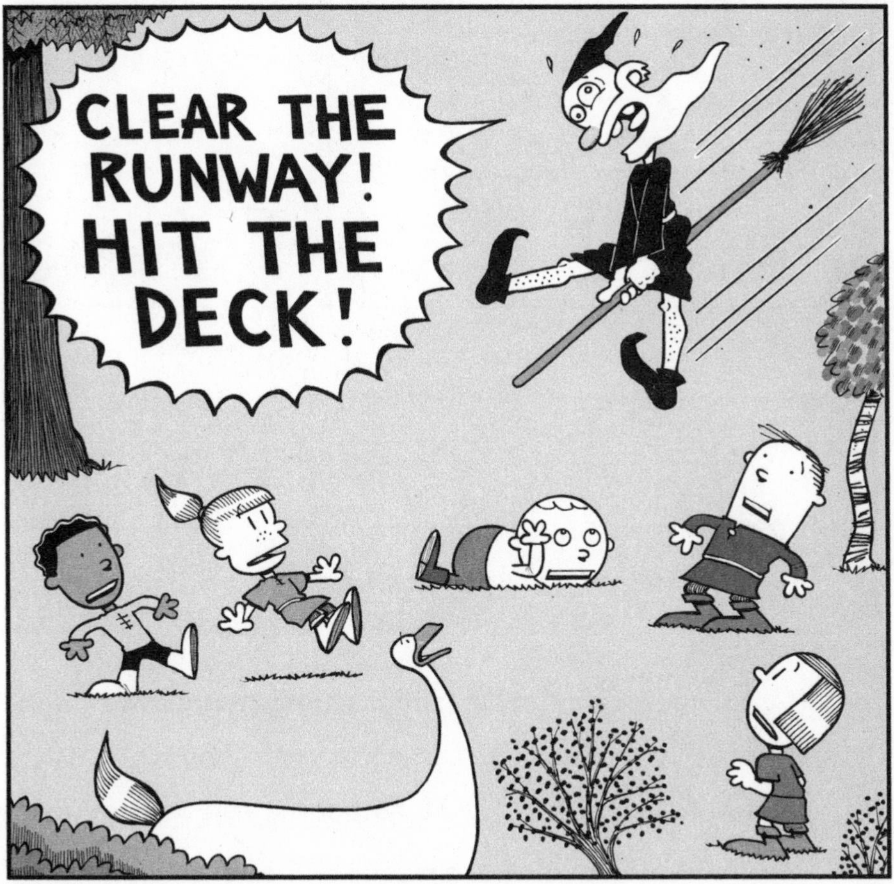
CLEAR THE RUNWAY! HIT THE DECK!

"M-my apologies for staring, young man," Mumblin stammers. "But you look like someone I once knew."

Conrad is beaming. "I AM someone you once knew. And I have missed you these last five years."

It's a joyous reunion. Mumblin can't wipe the astonished smile from his face. He listens eagerly to the tale of Conrad's long ordeal as Fendra's prisoner.

"Don't take this the wrong way," I tell him, "but your magical abilities seem to have ... uh ... improved!"

He smiles. "Yup! Finally got myself a new WAND!"

"A great deal, Your Majesty," Mumblin answers. "For one thing, Fendra has been employing a fiendish POTION to bewitch the citizens of the kingdom."

"We know," I say. "But how has she been able to pull it off?"

"By contaminating the water supply," Mumblin answers. "Every week, Gastley's soldiers have secretly spiked the kingdom's wells with a dose of Fendra's potion."

"Until THIS week!" Millie says with a smile.

Mumblin agrees. "Exactly. The potion's effects are weakening. And the people's devotion to King Gastley is beginning to crumble."

WONDERFUL! IT'S JUST AS WE HOPED!

THE NEWS ISN'T **ALL** GOOD, I'M AFRAID.

GADABOUT IS **MISSING!**

"MISSING?" we all cry in alarm.

"He recovered quickly once you sent him to me," Mumblin continues. "After he regained his strength, he said there was something he must do. He disappeared that very day."

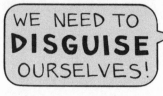

"Yes," he replies, "but it will do no good. Fendra has made certain of that."

"Then we'll do it the old-fashioned way!" Kevyn announces. "Follow me, everyone!"

He leads us down into the valley along a rugged trail that opens onto a patchwork of tidy fields. "My father comes to this farm often to tend to the horses," he explains.

THE FAMILY WHO LIVES HERE WON'T MIND IF WE BORROW THOSE **CLOAKS!**

PERFECT! THE HOODS WILL HELP TO HIDE YOUR FACES!

AS FOR THE **REST** OF US, THIS **WAGON** WILL PROVIDE OUR COVER!

WE'LL HIDE UNDER THE POTATOES...

...AND **YOU'LL** POSE AS **FARMERS** BRINGING YOUR CROP TO MARKET!

JOLLY GOOD!

"Look to the skies," Millie repeats. "I wonder what he means."

There's no time to think about it. Uncle Budrick helps Conrad hitch Dusty to the wagon, and the rest of us burrow deep under the mound of spuds. Then we start down the bumpy road toward the gates of Byjovia.

"Uh-oh. We've got a problem," Uncle Budrick warns as we draw closer. He brings the wagon to a sudden stop.

We start rolling again, and after a few minutes I hear the harsh voice of one of the soldiers.

"Fool!" snarls the first voice. "King Gastley is delivering a message of utmost importance. Attendance is mandatory."

"They're unarmed," the second guard announces after frisking Uncle Budrick and Conrad.

We pass through the gate and rattle along the cobblestone streets. I can't see a thing, but I can hear the brutal shouts of Gastley's soldiers herding people toward the market square.

The sound of a trumpet blast rises above the chaos. I wriggle toward the top layer of potatoes to sneak a look at the scene unfolding before us.

Gastley appears, and right away I can hear the proof that Fendra's spell is growing weaker: nobody applauds. Several of the king's soldiers are stationed around the square with swords drawn. The air feels thick with fear.

"People of Byjovia!" Gastley begins.

The crowd grows restless as Fendra slinks from the shadows, clutching a wand in her bony hand.

Two burly soldiers push their way through the mob, and between them is the prisoner. I try to get a better look, but the swirling masses of people block my view.

"Behold the condemned!" crows Gastley. "Earlier today, he was caught hosting a group of traitors in his stable!"

There's a muffled cry behind me. I turn to see Kevyn, his eyes wild with panic, alongside Simon and Millie. All four of us struggle to free ourselves. This is horrifying: Nolan's about to be put to death, and we're trapped in a pile of potatoes.

Gastley's speaking to Nolan now. "I can't stand idly by and watch you conspire against the crown, ostler," he drawls. "A king must be strong."

And now a figure in a hooded cloak strides to the front of the square. Standing shoulder to shoulder with Nolan, he gazes up at Gastley.

"Yes," a familiar voice booms, "surely, a king must be strong..."

An eerie hush instantly falls over the market square. It's as if all the people in Byjovia have lost their voices . . .

. . . and then found them again.

Conrad raises his hand, and the crowd goes quiet once more. Then he calmly addresses Gastley, whose face is a chalk-white mask of shock and rage.

"You're not fit to rule this kingdom," Conrad tells him. "And you have no right to take this man's life."

I WON'T **ALLOW** IT!

Gastley flashes an evil grin. "Very well, brother."

THEN **YOU'LL** DIE IN HIS **PLACE!**

DESTROY HIM.

ARE YOU CRAZY?

IF HE'S **DEAD,** WE CAN'T HARVEST HIS BLOOD FOR MY **POTION!**

"And that potion is what made you KING!"

"Yes," Gastley replies frostily. "And because I am king, I get to decide who lives and who dies."

I've finally managed to free myself from my potato prison. I leap off the wagon and bolt into the square where Conrad stands with Nolan. Frightened screams erupt from the crowd as Fendra lifts her wand. Come on, Max. MOVE!

There's only one thing to do: I lunge in front of Conrad, and . . .

KWANNG!

The beam of energy crashes into the blade like a lightning strike. I'm expecting it to knock the dagger from my hand, but I barely feel a thing—just a warm glow as the beam hits the metal, rebounds, and rockets back toward . . .

He looks ready to explode. His chest heaving, his eyes burning with fury, he shakes a finger at me. "You wretched brat! You very nearly assassinated your KING!"

I know this guy. He was in Gastley's throne room the night we broke Uncle Budrick out of the castle. But he was swinging an ax back then. This time, he's holding a sword.

Wait a minute. That SWORD! Isn't that—?

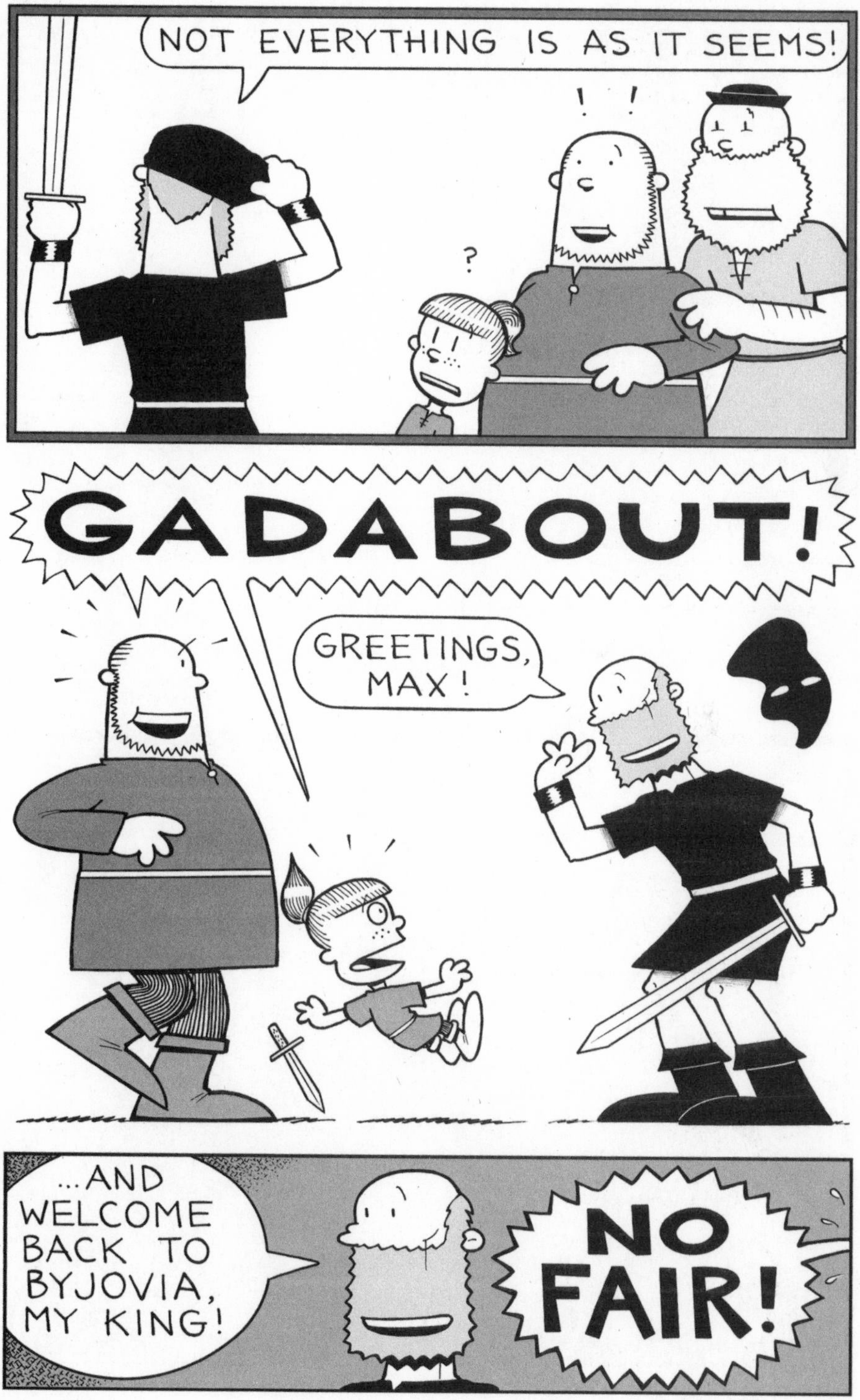
NOT EVERYTHING IS AS IT SEEMS!
! !
?
GADABOUT!
GREETINGS, MAX!
...AND WELCOME BACK TO BYJOVIA, MY KING!
NO FAIR!

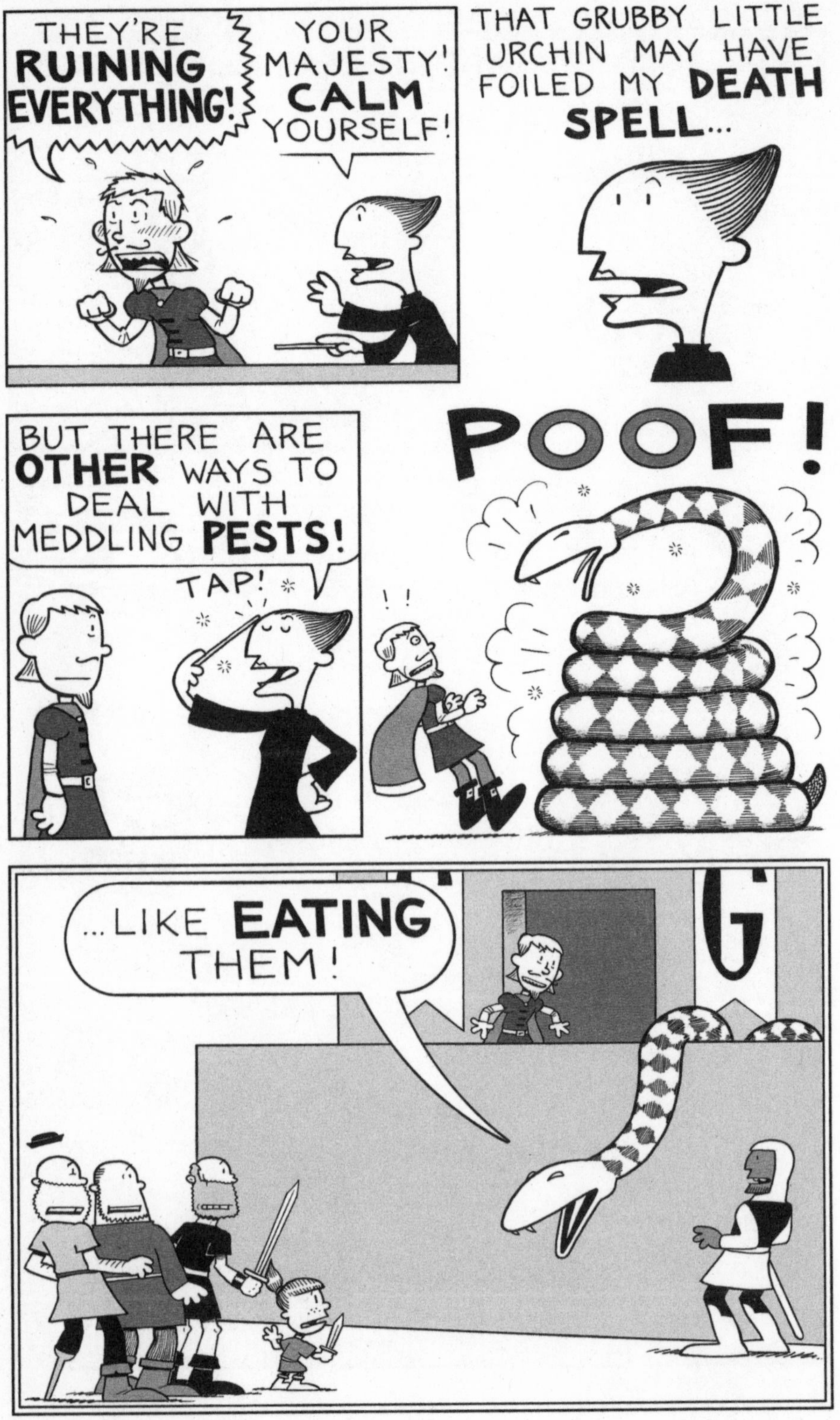
THEY'RE RUINING EVERYTHING!
YOUR MAJESTY! CALM YOURSELF!
THAT GRUBBY LITTLE URCHIN MAY HAVE FOILED MY DEATH SPELL...
BUT THERE ARE OTHER WAYS TO DEAL WITH MEDDLING PESTS!
TAP!
POOF!
...LIKE EATING THEM!
G

Fendra was scary enough as a witch. What do we do now that she's a GIANT SNAKE? As her immense body slithers across the cobblestones, Gadabout storms forward.

Fendra rises up, her red mouth gaping as she prepares to strike. But she never gets the chance. There's a blinding flash, a crackling beam of golden light, and . . .

Gastley stares in disbelief as the serpent collapses into dust. This is no magic trick. Fendra is history.

"YOU MISERABLE WORMS!!" he shrieks.

"Curse that gong," Gadabout hisses through gritted teeth. "It'll bring his soldiers running."

I hear the rhythmic stomping of heavy boots. Moments later, from the side streets and alleys, Gastley's men pour into the square, ready for battle.

"Uh . . . can we defeat a whole ARMY?" I ask.

"We won't have to," says Conrad, peering at the horizon.

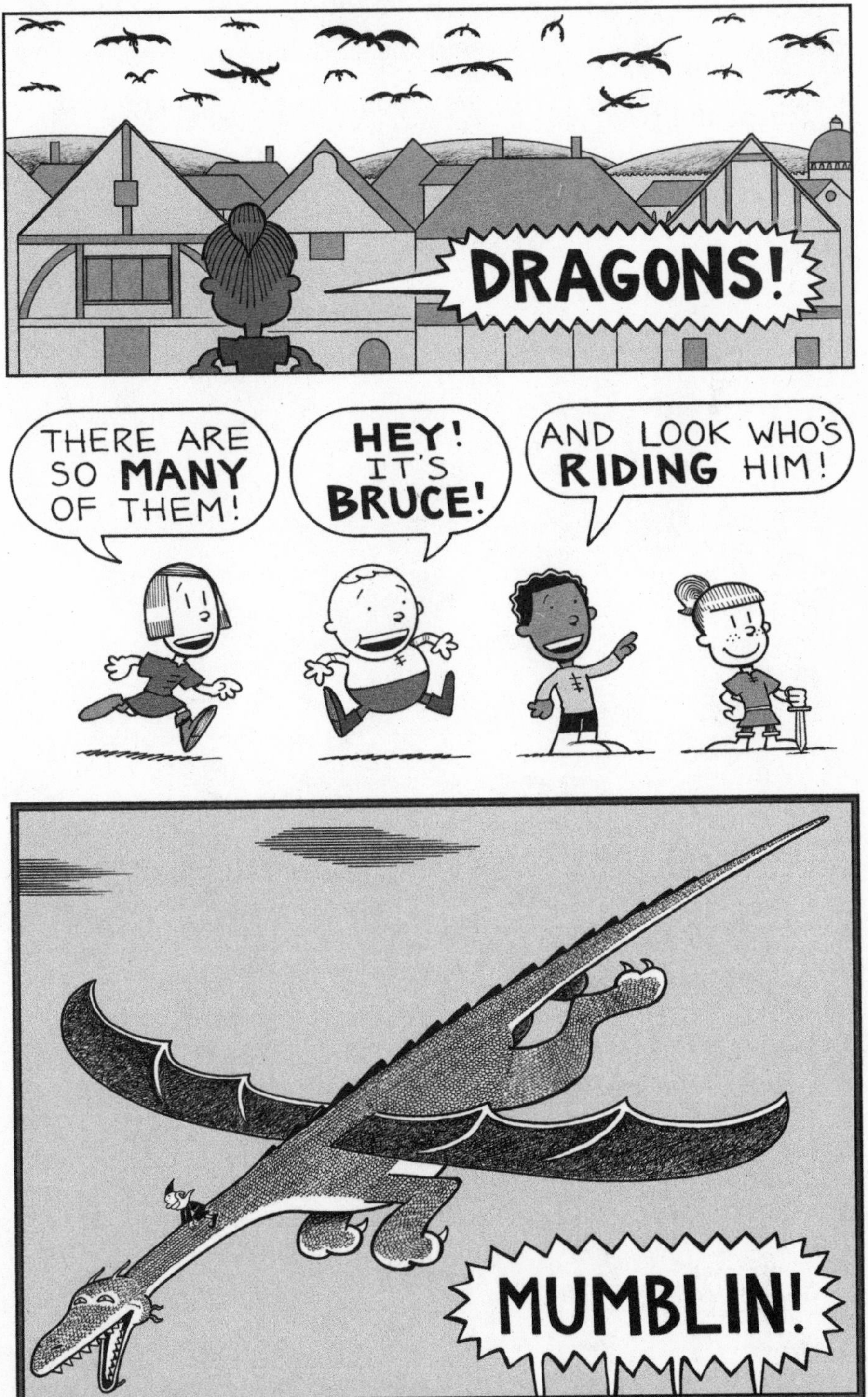
DRAGONS!
THERE ARE SO MANY OF THEM!
HEY! IT'S BRUCE!
AND LOOK WHO'S RIDING HIM!
MUMBLIN!

We all watch in amazement as Mumblin and his band of dragons swoop over the rooftops and into the square. The people are terrified—until they look more closely and realize there's nothing to fear.

It's the SOLDIERS the dragons have come for.

Bruce lands right beside us and nods in greeting. Mumblin slides off his back and drops nimbly to the ground.

"Thanks, ol' buddy," he says, patting Bruce's nose.

The dragon snorts and swings his head toward Gastley. The king — sorry, FORMER king — howls in terror.

With just a few beats of his mighty wings, Bruce climbs into the clouds and joins the host of dragons flying north. There are too many of them to count—and each one holds in its giant claws a pack of panicked soldiers. Gastley's screams echo, fade, and wither away in the shifting breeze. He's gone.

"It would be an honor, Millie," Mumblin says.

"I say yes," Conrad answers immediately. "Without Millie's cleverness and courage, our cause would surely have failed."

"From this day forward, all of Byjovia's children will choose their own paths in life—no matter where those paths may lead," the king declares.

Hey, did you see that? Not only do Simon and I get to be knights, but the two of us just invented the high five. Are we on a hot streak or WHAT?

"Well, Max, if you're going to knight school, then I'm getting out of the entertainment biz," Uncle Budrick says.

"I will make you the royal troubadour!" Conrad announces. "Instead of wandering to distant lands . . ."

No, neither will I. Believe me, I've tried. Anyway, I'm glad Uncle Budrick is sticking around. I'd miss him too much if he went back out on the circuit. He might not be the perfect uncle . . .

You know what's sort of crazy? I was about to say that Uncle Budrick is the only family I've got. But I should know better. That's not even CLOSE to true.

Kevyn hurries over, beaming with excitement. "It's just as the Book of Prophecies predicted, Max! You're a HERO!"

I notice my cheeks growing warm. "I'm not a hero," I say.

"I didn't even know what I was DOING half the time."

"You're too modest!" he exclaims. "Because of YOU, this is the start of a bright new chapter in Byjovian history!"

I look around the square at all the happy faces. People embrace. Bells ring out from the palace tower. "I see what you mean," I tell him. "What a day."

"Indeed!" Kevyn says with a smile. "What a day . . ."

Lincoln Peirce is a New York Times bestselling author and cartoonist. His comic strip *Big Nate*, featuring the adventures of an irrepressible sixth grader, appears in over 400 newspapers worldwide and online at gocomics.com/bignate. In 2010, he began a series of illustrated novels based on the strip, introducing Nate and his cast of classmates and teachers to a new generation of young readers. In the past seven years, sixteen million Big Nate books have been sold.

Max and the Midknights, Lincoln's first novel for Crown Books for Young Readers, originated as an unfinished spoof of sword and sorcery tales. Returning to the idea years later, Lincoln rewrote the story around Max, a ten-year-old apprentice troubadour who dreams of becoming a knight. The result is a high-spirited medieval adventure, supported by hundreds of dynamic illustrations employing the language of comics. Of the lively visual format that has become his trademark, Lincoln says, "I try to write the sort of books I would have loved reading when I was a kid."

When he is not writing or drawing, Lincoln enjoys playing ice hockey, doing crossword puzzles, and hosting a weekly radio show devoted to vintage country music. He and his wife, Jessica, have two children and live in Portland, Maine.